BILLIONAIRE'S BLACKMAIL BRIDE

JUDY ANGELO

THE BILLIONAIRE BROTHERS KENT
Book 3

BAD BOY BILLIONAIRES
Volume 1 - Tamed by the Billionaire
Volume 2 - Maid in the USA
Volume 3 - Billionaire's Island Bride
Volume 4 - Dangerous Deception
Volume 5 - To Tame a Tycoon
Volume 6 - Sweet Seduction
Volume 7 - Daddy by December
Volume 8 - To Catch a Man (in 30 Days or Less)
Volume 9 – Bedding her Billionaire Boss
Volume 10 - Her Indecent Proposal
Volume 11 - So Much Trouble When She Walked In
Volume 12 – Married by Midnight

THE BILLIONAIRE BROTHERS KENT
Book 1 - The Billionaire Next Door
Book 2 - Babies for the Billionaire
Book 3 - Billionaire's Blackmail Bride
Book 4 - Bossing the Billionaire

THE CASTILLOS
Book 1 - Beauty and the Beastly Billionaire
Book 2 – Training the Tycoon
Book 3 – The Mogul's Maiden Mistress
Book 4 – Eva and the Extreme Executive

HOLIDAY EDITIONS
Rome for the Holidays (Novella)
Rome for Always (Novel)

The NAUGHTY AND NICE Series
Volume 1 - **Naughty by Nature**

COMEDY, CONFLICT & ROMANCE Series
Book 1 - Taming the Fury
Book 2 - Outwitting the Wolf
Book 3 – Romancing Malone

JUDY ANGELO

COLLECTIONS

BAD BOY BILLIONAIRES, Coll. I - Vols. 1 - 4
BAD BOY BILLIONAIRES, Coll. II - Vols. 5 - 8
BAD BOY BILLIONAIRES, Coll. III - Vols. 9 - 12
BILLIONAIRE BROS. KENT - Books 1 - 4

Author contact:
www.judyangelo.com[1]
judyangeloauthor@gmail.com

---

1. http://www.judyangelo.com/

BILLIONAIRE'S BLACKMAIL BRIDE

As a research scientist it is **Lani Donatelli**'s dream to make a difference in the lives of people suffering from neurodegenerative diseases. There's only one problem, and it's a huge one - she's lost her funding from the big pharmaceutical companies and her research lab is in danger of closing down. Without funding her experiments are at a standstill. On top of that, she has one month to come up with the money to clear months of arrears with the leasing company before she and her team are evicted. In desperation, she turns to the one man she knows can save her skin. But is she willing to pay the price he demands?

As co-member of a Houston school board, **Ridge Kent** has admired Lani Donatelli for months. She, however, can't stand him. According to her, he's nothing but a joker and an annoying one at that. Their disagreements at board meetings don't help since the constant conflict builds a brick wall between them. He wants to get to know her better but how can he, when all their interactions have been the polar opposite of positive? And then, like a heaven-sent miracle, lovely little Lani falls right into his hands. She has nowhere to turn but to him. He is willing to help, on one condition - Lani Donatelli must become his wife.

Bride by blackmail - a recipe for disaster or an unexpected chance for love?

CHAPTER ONE

Sweet. The gods must be smiling down on him today. Lani Donatelli was sitting right here in his office and she was in big trouble. Could things go any better?

Leaning back in his chair, Ridge tented his fingers and regarded her through narrowed eyes. He was going to play tough even though he was laughing inside. She'd fallen right into his hands and he could not believe his luck.

"How's that again?" he asked, feigning confusion, watching the emotions flit across her face.

Lani gave an exasperated sigh. "Ridge Kent, you heard every word I said. Why should I repeat myself?" The color rising in her cheeks, Lani was clenching and unclenching her hands like she was trying hard not to hop out of her chair, reach across the desk and strangle him. She looked so cute when she was angry, like a little pink pixie, so tiny she could pass for a kid as she sat there, lost in the big, black office chair. And it didn't help that she was sporting a super-short boy haircut. If he didn't already know her he'd swear she was a stray twelve year old who'd wandered into his office.

But enough of admiring little Miss Cuteness. She'd asked a pointed question and he was only too willing to answer. "Maybe you should repeat yourself," he said, his tone cool, "because you really need this favor."

At his words Lani's eyes shot daggers and she looked like if she could have killed him with her glare she would have. "You don't need to rub it in," she said through clenched teeth.

"Oh, but I do," he replied. "I most certainly do."

"Jerk," she muttered under her breath.

But that didn't faze him at all. He knew exactly what he was doing. "I'm waiting," he said, just in case she needed a little more prompting.

Lani gave a heavy sigh then shook her head. "I'll go slower this time just so you'll understand. I've lost my funding for the research project I'm working on. A very important project. It's impossible for me to find alternative funding at such short notice and that's why I need your help."

"I see." Ridge leaned forward, holding her gaze. "And what's so important about this research project of yours? Why not shelve it and move on to something else?"

She looked at him like he was just short of being a blinking idiot. "Don't you get it? This is important. Life changing. It could make a difference in thousands of people's lives. You don't start a study that could make such an impact and then you shelve it. Are you crazy?"

For someone who'd come to his door begging she sure wasn't acting humble. The way she was speaking to him it was like he was the one who needed the favor, not her. Ridge had to hold in a chuckle. He kept his face serious as he asked the next question. "So if your project is that important why can't you get funding? Isn't this the sort of thing those big pharmaceutical companies want to be involved in?"

Lani grimaced. "Not this one. I'm not doing research on a synthetic drug, something they can patent. My research is on natural plant alternatives so they don't give a damn. If you can't make billions off it they don't want to hear about it."

"I see," he said again, nodding slowly as he pondered her words. "So what you're saying is, you want me to invest in a project for which there is no return. The pharmaceutical companies won't do it so why should I?"

"Why should... is that all you ever think about? How much money you stand to make?"

Her scowl was so dark Ridge was having a hard time keeping a straight face. God, he was having fun pushing her buttons.

He shrugged. "I'm a businessman," he said, his tone nonchalant. "If you ain't makin' money you ain't got no business."

That got her good. He could see it in the way her teeth clenched and her eyes narrowed. "Well, if that's the position you're going to take it looks like I came to the wrong person." She slapped her hands on the arms of her chair and hopped to her feet. "Thanks for nothing. Good day, Mr. Kent." Then she turned and stalked off toward the door.

Ridge waited until her hand was on the knob and then he spoke. "Come back here, Miss Donatelli." His voice was firm and curt. "Come back and sit down," he paused for maximum effect, "or else you're not getting a cent out of me."

She froze, hand still on the knob, and then slowly she turned and stared back at him. Eyes narrowed, she frowned. "So you're giving me the money?"

Ridge gave her a crooked grin. "I might. But there's just one thing."

Her frown deepened and, moving slowly, she folded her arms in front of her. "What," she said slowly, the word dripping with suspicion, "thing?"

She was curious now, and wary, but he wasn't going to make things that easy. Lani would have to learn that he was the one holding the blade and she'd better tread carefully.

"I'll tell you," he said, his tone frigid, "as soon as you find your butt back in your chair."

He saw her quick look of surprise at his imperious tone but in a flash it was gone. Now her ebony eyes glinted with unmistakable anger. It was obvious she wanted to tell him to go to hell but she was too smart for that. Her mind was ticking fast and he could see the second that she decided to suck it up and do what he'd ordered. She was a proud and independent woman but she wasn't stupid.

With a twist of her lips she released her arms and marched back to the chair she'd just vacated. It was a good thing she was wearing slacks and not a dress because she practically flung herself down into it, her expression telling him that whatever it was he had to say to her, she was not looking forward to it.

"So what 'thing' is it you want to tell me," she said, "before you give me the money?"

Ridge didn't answer. He'd been planning to make her a friendly proposition, one she could live with, but screw that. Little Miss Lani was being a bit too haughty for his liking...even though she was the one asking favors. Time to take her down a notch or two.

"I'll give you the money," he said, his eyes never leaving hers, "on one condition."

Lani drew in a slow breath and her gaze grew even more suspicious. "What condition?"

"You can get your money to do your precious research project," he said, his tone even, "as long as you agree to marry me. I want you to be my wife for a year."

That declaration didn't get him the reaction he'd been expecting. Instead of the shock and horror he'd anticipated Lani did the very opposite. The contrary girl burst out laughing.

"I heard you could be a joker but this takes the cake. So you're a businessman turned comedian now?" She wasn't shy with her guffaws. She was laughing so hard Ridge was thinking she might pitch forward and fall out of her chair.

But he wouldn't say a word. He would let her have her moment of fun and then he would set her straight. That grin would be wiped from her face soon enough.

When she finally calmed down enough to stop laughing and slide back in her chair Ridge got up and walked over to the credenza on top of which sat an ice bucket with bottles of water and juice. He glanced over at her. "Want one?" he asked.

She shook her head.

With a shrug he turned, grabbed a bottle of water and tipped it to his lips. He downed a third of it in one swig. As he lowered the bottle and replaced the cap he regarded her with casual interest. "Ready to talk to me now?"

"About what?" she asked, a smile teasing the corner of her mouth. "Of course you weren't serious."

He gave her a slow smile. "I'm dead serious."

It was only then that things seemed to sink in for Lani. The smile that had tickled her mouth disappeared. The lips that had just curled so prettily now turned thin and firm. "But why?" she asked, her tone half combative, half confused. "Why would you want me to marry you? We don't even like each other."

And the way she said the last sentence, curling her lips like the very thought repulsed her, made him even more determined to stick to his guns. He would bring her to heel if it killed him.

"Let's just say I've got my reasons." He spoke calmly, not giving away the fact that she'd just pissed him off. There would be time enough to get his revenge for that transgression.

"But I don't get it." As he walked back to his desk her eyes followed him, boring into him, never letting him go. He definitely had her attention now. "Ever since we met," she continued, "we've been at loggerheads. In fact, I wouldn't even be in your office right now if I weren't desperate."

Ridge smiled. "That, little Lani, is the operative word. The question is, how desperate are you?" He made sure to put emphasis on the word just so she didn't miss the point.

Lani's breathing was growing more and more agitated by the minute. Nostrils flaring, she got up and out of the chair and stood there, hands clenched at her sides. "You're sick. You know that?"

His smile deepened. "I may be," he said, his tone relaxed as ever, "but you're the one who's going to make this decision. Not me."

With a shrug he sank back into his chair and looked at the seething woman standing in front of his desk. "My condition is on the table, Lani. Take it or leave it."

***

Lani couldn't believe the pickle she was in. Worse, she couldn't believe her only way out might be to consider Ridge Kent's insane proposal. Marry him just so she could get funding for her research? He must be mad.

When he'd laid down his condition she'd stormed out of his office, slamming the door shut behind her. Then she'd gone straight to the research lab and put in six more hours of work even though that had her leaving at minutes after ten o'clock. She'd been so worked up she couldn't have slept even if she'd tried and so she'd worked into the late hours of the night. By the time she quit and went home she was exhausted.

But if she'd thought making herself super tired would ensure a night of deep sleep she was sadly mistaken. After a long night of fitful sleep she dragged herself out of bed and readied herself for another busy day. And thanks to Ridge she felt as beat up as an old jalopy. Great.

After a quick shower and some cereal Lani grabbed her bag and jacket then headed for the elevator. She'd just exited the underground parking garage and was driving away from her apartment building when her cell phone rang. "Lani, where are you? I stopped at The Breakfast Klub and got you a Katfish and Grits meal. You're gonna get here soon?"

"Just heading out," she said as she turned onto South Heights Boulevard. "Be there in fifteen minutes."

As she hung up from her assistant Lani sighed. Chris was as good as it got when it came to assistants – dedicated, focused and always ready to go the extra mile. She only hoped she wouldn't have to let him go. But if they ran out of money what else could she do? She was the only one who knew it but the research lab was this close to being closed down.

When she got to the lab Chris had already set up the test tubes and Bunsen burners and was busy washing beakers in the sink. As she came in he turned. "Hey, boss. What took you so long? Your food's getting cold." Then he frowned and a look of concern crossed his face. "You don't look so good. Are you all right?"

She grimaced. "I'm okay. Just tired, that's all. I didn't sleep so good last night." She shrugged out of her jacket and donned her lab coat. "And the traffic this morning didn't help, either. Why is traffic always so tight in Houston? I hate Westheimer Road."

Chris grimaced. "I avoid it like the plague, especially at this time of year. Don't you know March is the worst month to want to be on that road? Too many tourists in town for the rodeo."

Lani rolled her eyes. "Now he tells me." Then she walked over to look at the Petri dishes on the long table against the back wall. She stared at her specimens for a while then, growing thoughtful, she put her finger to her chin. "We haven't made much progress with these cultures," she said to no-one in particular. "I just hope we haven't wasted the last three weeks."

"But we can't go any further until you get some more plant samples, remember?" Of course, Chris had to remind her about something she already knew, so his stating the obvious didn't help her any.

"Yeah," she said with a sigh. "But that comes with a price tag." It was a price they couldn't afford. She didn't bother telling him that part.

As lead researcher and director of Allied Labs it was her job to worry about where the money was going to come from to pay for plant supplies, the equipment, the salaries and all the overseas trips that would be required to source the supplies. Beside herself, she had Chris and Minerva to worry about. Even though Minerva was part-time her wages were still a strain on the already meager budget. But right now she didn't even want to think about that. She had a long day ahead of her and she was already depressed. There was no sense in making things worse by dwelling on the problems.

"Okay, young man," she said with forced cheeriness, "let's see what we can do to save this experiment."

At her words Chris smiled and Lani knew why. Even though she called him young man, at twenty-nine she was not much older than Chris. In fact, when they attended meetings people often thought he was the one in charge. With her short boy haircut and her penchant for shirts and trousers she could pass for his little brother. And the fact that he was on the heavy side made him look older than his twenty-seven years.

Instead of taking offense at the frequent misunderstanding Lani just laughed it off. It was always so comical when they realized she was the one with the doctorate degrees in botany and neuroscience. It never failed to crack her up when the serious-looking corporate heads did a double-take when they found they wouldn't get answers to their questions unless they talked to her.

But now the sad truth was, all her qualifications didn't mean a thing if she didn't find a way to continue conducting her experiments. She could feel that she was heading for a breakthrough. In her research on degenerative diseases such as Parkinson's, Alzheimer's Disease and multiple sclerosis she had the unusual advantage of an extensive knowledge of the diseases as well as the possible treatments that the plant world could provide. She wanted to use her training in botany and neuroscience to explore alternatives to the current treatment options, many of which came with serious side effects.

She was even considering the ways in which her research could be of benefit in areas such as mental illness. Current treatments provided some relief to victims of the most serious of mental illnesses, schizophrenia. At the same time, long-term use altered the brain in such a way that some patients ended up with tardive dyskinesia, a disorder which had them making uncontrollable involuntary movements such as facial grimacing and tongue thrusting. Of course, this proved embarrassing and typically caused them considerable distress. The way Lani saw it, if she could find an alternative for such patients, one that would eliminate this condition, then this was one of the many areas in which her painstaking research would be well worth it.

The thought had hardly settled in her mind when the door burst open and Minerva, energetic as ever, bounced in. "Hey, Lani. Hey, Chris." She sent her shoulder bag sailing onto the low table by the entrance. "Here you go," she said, holding out a stack of envelopes to Lani as she dropped her aluminum water bottle onto the nearby shelf. "I got the mail."

"Thanks, Min." Lani took the envelopes but it was with a heavy heart. The chances were good that more than half of them were bills.

"No prob." Minerva headed toward the sink where she began to wash her hands. "I can't stay late today," she said as she scrubbed. "I've got a doctor's appointment."

"You okay?" Chris looked up from the dish into which he'd been peering.

"Yeah," Minerva said, tossing her head to get the shock of jet-black hair out of her eyes. "I just need to go get a shot. At my other job, apparently you've got to have all your immunizations up-to-date or they've got a problem." She rolled her eyes. "It's like they think I'm going to infect them or something."

Chris gave a snort of a laugh. "I wonder if all those tattoos and piercings have anything to do with it?"

Minerva jammed a fist on her hip. "It better not or else they'll have a lawsuit on their hands. That's discrimination."

While Chris and Minerva chattered away Lani was busy opening the envelopes. So far so good. She was on envelope number three and all she'd seen were a newsletter, a credit card solicitation and a bank statement that was so depressing she barely spared it a glance. But envelope number four, that was the killer. It was from the company from which she'd leased the building and before she even opened it she knew what it would say inside.

Gritting her teeth, Lani went ahead and opened it anyway. "Pursuant to my letter dated February 15, this is to advise that your rent is now two months in arrears. If payment is not made within seven days of the date of this letter proceedings will be instigated to regain possession of the property and recover all outstanding amounts, including fees. In order to avoid this, please make arrangement to immediately make payment in full."

Despite herself, the hand that held the letter trembled. She'd expected a reprimand, definitely a warning, but not this. Seven days to find two months' rent plus fees? Where in heaven's name was she going to get that kind of money?

She knew she was at fault for paying the salaries – excluding hers – before taking care of the rent but Chris was a father with two young children. How could she tell him she wasn't going to pay him this month? And Minerva was working two jobs to put her little sister through college. How could she dash that dream?

Now, though, it seemed she would have to. She'd gone without a salary for two months just to make ends meet but even that hadn't been enough. Without new funding the bank account had quickly run dry and even though she'd promised the leasing company she would catch up on the arrears within three months it was now obvious they weren't going to wait any longer. And who could blame them? When she'd made the promise she'd been sure something would have come in. Now, over a dozen meetings later, nothing. Now she knew it had all been wishful thinking on her part.

"You okay, boss? You don't look so good." Minerva had turned toward her, a slight frown on her face.

For the second time that morning Lani found she had to explain herself to a member of her team. "I'm... fine, Minerva. Just some business I have to take care of."

And as she said the words Lani's mind crept back to her meeting of the day before. Before he would give her any money Ridge Kent wanted her to be his wife. But only for one year. She guessed she could manage...as long as they had a little talk first and she'd laid down the rules of this engagement. Under the circumstances she could see no other way out of her dilemma.

And so, that conclusion reached, she made up her mind. She would do it. She would marry Ridge Kent. And, with all the wolves that were snarling at her door, the sooner the better.

CHAPTER TWO

"So what do you think?"

Ridge watched Rafe's face, trying to judge his reaction. His brother was all of six years younger than he was, only twenty-eight, but he had a good head set on his shoulders. More important than that, he was good at taking risks and winning. He had the nose for that sort of thing.

Rafe cocked an eyebrow at him. "You're asking me for advice? What about Ransom? He's the big brother, advice giver and everything rolled into one. Why don't you ask him what he thinks?"

Ridge gave him a cutting glare. "Because, dear brother, I don't want to ask Ransom. And I don't want to ask Ryder either so don't even go there." Leaning forward, he rested his elbows on his desk. "When you were trying to get Anya you asked me for help. Now it's your turn to tell me what you think will work." Then he chuckled. "You're the one who always prided himself on knowing tons of women and how they think. So what should I do about Lani?"

"Oh, Jeez." Rafe exhaled and put his hands on top of his head, his fingers interwoven and his elbows sticking out to the sides. "I never tried blackmailing a woman before. You got me with that one, Ridge." He lowered his hands and then he, too, was leaning forward. "And I'm a married man now so all that talk about me knowing lots of women, just keep it on the down-low, will you? That kind of stuff's behind me now."

"Yeah, sure." Ridge shrugged. "Anya won't hear it from me. But that still doesn't help me with my situation. Lani turned me down flat, bro. Walked out the door and never looked back. Looks like it's time for me to draw for plan B." He grimaced. "The only thing is, I don't have one."

"Hey, bud. Don't you know you've got a wild card?" Rafe was looking at him like he was slow. "You're in the oil business. Tell her that. Money talks. Don't you know that?"

Ridge shook his head. Now it was his turn to look at his brother like he was slow. "Did you hear what I said?" he asked. "I already offered her money, enough money to cover the cost of her research and her lab for more than a year. She turned me down cold."

"Not good enough," Rafe said drily. "Give her an extra half-a-million on top of that and you'll be good to go."

Not liking the sound of that, Ridge frowned. "I don't know," he said slowly. "That smacks of all-out bribery."

"So what do you call the offer you made her before?" Rafe shrugged. "Same thing but with the extra half-a-mil you're sweetening the pot. She won't just be covering her expenses. She'll have some money to spend on herself."

Ridge shook his head. "That would only make things worse. If you knew Lani you'd have figured that out."

"And that's the thing," Rafe said, getting up from his chair and walking over to the big bay window. "I don't know this Lani of yours. How come I never heard about her before now?"

"Because," Ridge said slowly, "she and I have never been...romantically involved."

Rafe's eyes narrowed and he turned to face Ridge. "Then why the hell do you want to get married to her?"

Ridge grimaced. He drew in a deep breath then let it out. "It's hard to explain."

Rafe gave him an impatient look. "Try me."

For a moment Ridge didn't reply but then he decided to spill it. "Her name's Lani Donatelli. She's a big-time research scientist who runs a lab. Allied Labs, it's called."

Rafe looked intrigued. "Since when did you run in those circles? A research scientist?"

Peeved by his brother's disdainful tone, Ridge made sure to set him straight. "We both happen to be members of the Houston North Academy school board. I fund some of their extra-curricular programs and she's their advisor for the science programs. I've known her for almost a year."

"And you've been lusting after her ever since, I bet." Rafe was grinning now.

"Why doesn't your crudity surprise me?" Ridge shook his head. "Anyway, the important thing is, I kind of like her."

"Kind of?"

"Okay, I'm attracted to her. A lot. It's just that she's never given me the time of day." He sighed. "And it doesn't help that we haven't seen eye-to-eye on a few issues being dealt with by the school board."

"So you've been pissing her off, huh?"

"You could say that."

Rafe chuckled. "No wonder you've had to resort to blackmail."

Ridge gave him an exasperated look. "Yeah, well not all of us were blessed with your gift of gab."

"The ladies call it charm," Rafe said, looking way too pleased with himself.

Ridge didn't bother answering that one. Instead, he went right to the heart of the problem. "So what's your suggestion, Mr. Expert? I called you here for advice. Now give it."

Rafe was smiling as he walked over and dropped back down onto the chair. "You know what, big brother? It feels good to have you coming to me for advice for a change. After all those years of you trying to bully me and boss me around I'm in the driver's seat now."

"Trying?" Ridge scoffed. "I bossed you around because you were the runt of the family and you still are. Don't you forget it." The kid had grown pretty tall, topping out at six foot three, but he was still no match for Ridge who bested him by an inch, not to mention forty more pounds.

"Yeah, but a runt who's got the key to solving your problem," Rafe said, looking like he didn't give a damn what Ridge had just said. "Right now you're desperate so I'm the one in charge."

"Is that right?" Ridge regarded him with a cool stare.

"That's right," Rafe said, "so listen up." He straightened up then sat forward in his chair. "Now here's what we'll do-"

A call came over the speaker phone, cutting him off. "You have a visitor, Mr. Kent." His assistant's voice came in, clear and crisp. "Miss Lani Donatelli."

Surprised, Ridge glanced over at Rafe just as his brother raised his eyebrows. "Bring her in," he told Miss Poole.

"I think that's my cue to exit," Rafe said and got up out of his chair.

"Wait." Ridge got up, too. "What's the idea you had for plan B?"

Rafe shrugged. "That's irrelevant now. The lady's already here. Improvise."

And with that he turned on his heel and walked to the door just as it opened and Lani stepped in.

"Good day, Miss Donatelli," Rafe said with a smile and a polite nod, making her eyes widen in surprise. Then, before she could respond, he went through the door and closed it firmly behind him.

Still standing by the door, Lani gave Ridge a look of puzzlement.

"My brother," Ridge said then waved her over to a chair. "He heard your name when Miss Poole announced you."

"Oh." Lani relaxed visibly. "For a moment there I thought you'd been discussing me or something."

Ridge cocked an eyebrow. "Now why would you think that?"

"I don't know. I just..." She shook her head. "Anyway, that's not important. What's important is why I came to see you."

Ridge watched as she settled in her chair then, his thoughts racing, he walked back to his desk but he did not retake his seat. Instead, he perched his rear on the edge of the desk and as he stared at her he folded his arms. "And why did you come to see me, Miss Donatelli?"

For just a fraction of a second tough little Lani looked hesitant, like she was afraid to say whatever it was she'd come to tell him. But then he saw her set her lips in a tight line and when she looked back at him her dark eyes flashed and she did not drop her gaze.

"I came to see you, Mr. Kent, to tell you that I will marry you." Her brows furrowed and she raised her hand to point an imperious finger at him. "But only for one year and not a day more. Do you understand?"

Ridge stared back at her, his look deliberately serious, but inside he was laughing. The way Lani was talking anybody would think she was the one in control of this situation. She was like a little terrier trying to assert its authority over a Mastiff.

After staring her down for a few seconds longer Ridge gave her a slow smile. "I'm glad you came around, Lani. Now go get yourself in order. We're getting married next weekend."

CHAPTER THREE

"I'm still amazed. How did you pull this off so fast?" Marie Donatelli straightened Lani's veil one more time. "A full-scale wedding in two weeks? How is that even possible?"

"I keep telling you, Mom, I had nothing to do with it. It was Ridge's team that pulled it all together." She wrinkled her nose. "I guess all things are possible as long as you have the money."

Marie smiled. "Well, it certainly helps."

"Yeah, it does, doesn't it?" Lani's words came out more as a grumble than a compliment. It was so unfair. The money had come so easy for this event – and Lani knew Ridge was spending thousands – but when it came to finding money for research that could make a huge difference in people's lives, she couldn't get any. Unless, of course, she married a man who was an expert at working her last nerve. How she would survive a year with him, she had no idea.

Marie stepped back, her brown eyes glistening as she gazed at her daughter. "You look so beautiful," she murmured, her voice cracking. "The perfect bride."

Lani frowned. "Mom, are you crying? Don't tell me you're getting emotional over this. I told you, it's just an arrangement. We'll be going our separate ways in a year." Then she gave Marie a cheeky grin. "Or less, if I'm lucky."

"I know your situation is a bit...unorthodox...but it's a wedding. My daughter's wedding. I can't help it if I get choked up."

"Just try and hold it in," Lani said drily. "Please."

Marie sighed. "I'll try, honey, but I'm not promising anything. You know me."

Lani shook her head but she didn't answer. Yes, she knew her mother well, like how she would tear up at the drop of a hat. Her mom cried over commercials, for goodness sake.

"But do you know what?" Marie continued. "Maybe it's a good thing this is happening. You were always so focused on your studies and then on your work, you haven't paid much attention to your social life."

Lani gave Marie a crooked smile. "You seem to know a lot about my social life."

"I do," Marie said with absolutely no hesitation. "You're twenty-nine, Lani. It's time you started thinking about your future."

"I am thinking about my future. That's why I work so hard."

Marie gave an exasperated sigh. "Let me put this another way. It's time you started thinking about my future which, I hope, will include grandbabies."

Lani laughed. "Mom, you're asking for grandkids already? You're only fifty-five. You're not like Dad, who's already retired. You're a busy woman. Where would you have time for grandchildren?"

"Don't you worry about that. All I want is for you to start thinking about family. You're not getting any younger. Remember that."

Lani didn't bother answering. It was no use reminding her mother that this wasn't a real marriage, only a temporary arrangement that would be over in a year. When she'd first told her about it, instead of expressing shock that her daughter would even consider such an arrangement she'd looked relieved, like she was glad there was finally hope for Lani. At the news, her father had simply shrugged and said, "You do what you have to do." She had such weird parents.

The only sane one had been her sister. Three years older than Lani, she'd always acted like she was a surrogate mom, dispensing advice like it was her purpose in life. Of course, she'd had lots to say about the 'arrangement'. She hadn't liked the idea, not one bit, and she'd told Lani so. But Lani had made up her mind and she wasn't about to change because Paula said so. It wasn't like she ever followed her sister's advice anyway.

And just as the thought crossed her mind the door swung open and Paula stuck her head inside. "Come on, Lani. We're ready for you. Dad's already at the front, waiting to give you away."

Those words made Lani's heart flip over but she straightened her back and drew in a steadying breath. Then, as her sister held the door wide open, she walked out.

"Well, here goes nothing," she muttered under her breath.

***

"You pulled this one out of a hat," Ransom said, peering into the mirror as he straightened his bow tie. "Where've you been hiding the little lady?"

"Oh, around," Ridge said casually as he relaxed on the sofa and watched as his older brother finished his titivation then turned toward him. "We've known each other about a year." He wasn't prepared to say much more than that. He'd already spilled his guts to Rafe. He wasn't about to give his other brothers reason to start bugging him. Rafe was a risk-taker so he was cool but Ransom and Ryder? Too uptight for anybody's good.

Ryder, who'd propped his butt against the stool by the breakfast bar, was watching Ridge with an amused smile. "I still can't believe this is happening. You're such a joker, when you told me you were getting married in two weeks I thought this was one of your usual pranks and I told Mom so. Boy, you proved me wrong this time."

"And nearly gave Mom a heart attack in the process," Rafe said with a chuckle. "For days she was running around like a chicken without a head."

"But I told her I was handling everything," Ridge said. "It wasn't like I needed her help in planning this thing. I had my team taking care of everything."

"Yeah, but you know Mom," Rafe said with a shrug. "Everything's got to be just right."

"Miss Perfectionist," Ryder said in agreement. "But it's a good thing, since Dad's such a sloppy organizer."

Ransom smiled. "Opposites attract." He jerked his chin toward Ridge. "That the case with you and Lani?"

Ridge grimaced. "Maybe. She doesn't seem to find my jokes all that funny."

"Jokes," Ryder asked, his tone skeptical, "or pranks?"

Ridge shrugged. "Whatever." But then he thought about it. "It would be kind of great if she had more of a sense of humor."

Instead of agreeing, Ransom shook his head. "Be careful what you wish for. You just might get it." Then he jerked his head toward the door. "Come on, guys. Time to go make a good man out of this beast." And, not even waiting for them to make a move, Ridge's best man strode out of the suite, leaving the rest of them to follow.

Later he made up for his nonchalant behavior, though. As Ridge stood at the front of the church waiting for his bride, sweat beading his forehead and his upper lip, it was Ransom who dabbed his face with a folded handkerchief. He even whispered a few supportive words that helped Ridge calm down a bit.

He had no idea he would have gotten so nervous just because he was attending a little old wedding. His own, but still. If he'd known it would be so nerve-wracking maybe he would have ditched the whole idea and just gone in front of a judge with a couple of witnesses. But the really weird thing was, he had no idea what he was so nervous about. After all, it was just Lani, right?

And then he saw her. She was standing there at the entrance, her hand on the arm of a stately-looking gentleman with graying hair. The look in the man's eyes told Ridge that he was the proud 'give-away' father. But it wasn't that gentleman who made Ridge's heart jerk in his chest. When Lani looked away from her father and turned to face front Ridge's breath caught in his throat. She was more beautiful than he'd ever seen her. Even through the diaphanous veil that covered her face he could see the soft petals of her rose-red lips and the brilliant sparkle of her onyx eyes. The veil she was wearing was held in place atop her head by a circular band decorated by a garland of tiny white flowers. As tiny as she was beside her very tall papa it made her look like a bewitching little fairy, so exquisitely beautiful he couldn't tear his eyes away.

Then, as if she hadn't entranced him enough, she started down the aisle on her father's arm, moving with such style and grace that he couldn't have pulled his eyes away if his life depended on it. Since the day he met her Ridge knew Lani was beautiful but was this the same woman who seemed to wear nothing but slacks and loafers? In heels that were so high he feared for her safety Lani practically floated up the aisle, her poise making all heads turn in obvious admiration.

And then she was standing there right in front of him, so close that he was soon losing himself in the shimmering dark pools of her eyes. Like she could see the tension in him, her lips curled in a smile that had him drawing in a deep breath. God, he wanted to kiss her. So bad.

But like a good little boy he didn't pull her into his arms and kiss her breathless like he wanted to. Instead he smiled down at her and then reached out and lifted the veil from her face, exposing her loveliness to his eager gaze. Close up she was even more beautiful. He must have been staring at her too long and too hard because Lani took his hands and gave them a gentle squeeze, bringing him back to awareness.

The officiant cleared his throat and with that the ceremony began. "Dearly beloved, we're gathered here today to witness and celebrate the union of Leilani Isabella Donatelli and Coleridge Martin Kent." The man's voice rose, filling the room, and as he spoke the words Ridge held Lani's hands and gazed deep into her eyes.

"Today you enter as individuals but you leave as man and wife," he continued, "blending together, becoming as one, moving on to the greatest of all social interactions, the uniting of body, mind and spirit."

As the words flowed from his lips the minister waxed loquacious, moving on from celebrating the union of the couple to dispensing advice on the keys to a successful marriage.

And all that time Ridge was dying for him to get to the best part.

It wasn't going to come that fast, though. First, he had to suffer through a series of readings. "Marriage is not just the joining of hands," the man admonished. "It is the joining of hearts. It is a union built on commitment and support."

Even as he smiled down at his wife-to-be Ridge gritted his teeth, wanting the man to get on with it. The readings were meaningful but there were so many of them. Two he could stomach, but five? Ridge could only hope Lani wasn't picking up on his agitation.

And then it was time for them to exchange vows. Ridge almost breathed an audible sigh of relief.

"Do you, Coleridge Kent, take Leilani Donatelli to be your partner for life, promising to care for her, honor and respect her, to console her in times of sorrow and support her in all her endeavors?"

Without hesitation Ridge gave his response. "I do."

"And do you, Leilani Donatelli..."

As the words were repeated Lani lifted her face to Ridge, her lips curling into a soft smile. "I do," she said, her voice bold and clarion-clear, carrying throughout the church.

"The ring, please."

Now it was time for Ridge to put his seal on the woman who'd started by turning him down flat. Thank goodness she'd come around.

And then, finally, came the part Ridge had been waiting for the whole time.

"By the power vested in me by the State of Texas I now pronounce you husband and wife. You may kiss your bride."

Smiling in satisfaction, Ridge looked down at his bride and then he reached for her, eager to taste her lips. This first kiss would be in front of an audience but he wasn't complaining. He would take it any way he could get it. Knowing Lani, he might not get another chance for a while.

Bending low, Ridge captured her lips in a kiss meant to show her she was his, body and soul. He'd thought she would be shy, would even resist, but she surprised him by responding willingly, even eagerly. The fact that she had an audience didn't seem to bother her, not one bit.

When he finally let her go Lani came off her tiptoes and settled back down on her heels but she did not release his gaze. She was smiling and she was staring boldly back at him, a hint of mischief in her eyes.

And, for some strange reason, at the look in her eyes a tiny tingle of worry ran up his spine.

CHAPTER FOUR

Tonight was Lani's wedding night and she could hardly wait. But it was not for the reason most people would imagine. No, she had plans for a night that promised to be a lot of fun. Fun for her, anyway. For Ridge Kent, not so much.

Ridge had blackmailed her into marrying him and she'd ended up accepting his proposal, if you could call it that. It was like no marriage proposal she would ever have expected. In fact, she'd pretty much given up on being proposed to at all. Her work had been her life for so many years. She'd hardly had time to include a man in the middle of that. And then, before she knew it, she was pushing thirty and her mother had begun harassing her for grandkids.

Now her mother finally had her wish. Her daughter was a married woman and no amount of explaining would make her see there was really no cause for celebration. Her heart was set on grandkids, temporary arrangement be damned.

But that wasn't going to happen, not if Lani had anything to do with it. And she did. A lot.

She smiled as she thought back to the conversation she'd had with Ridge just days before the wedding.

"There will be no love-making," she'd declared, laying down the rule before he got any ideas. "No sex or anything even close."

He'd given her a sly grin. "What about something that's just in the ball park?"

"No, nothing. Zilch." She chopped her hand down with force, showing him just how much she meant the zilch part. "No hugging, no kissing, nada."

"Hmm. Kinda harsh, aren't we?" For some reason he hadn't seemed worried. Sort of amused, really. Did he think she didn't mean it? "So," he continued, "for one whole year we're going to live in the same house and not touch each other? Do you really think you can manage that?"

Then his grin widened and he spread his arms wide. "How are you going to resist all this, what do you ladies call it, man candy?"

"Ha. Don't get ahead of yourself. I'll resist you just fine. You just give me your promise that we won't make love."

He'd come close, right up to her, and when he spoke his voice was deceptively cool. "Here's what I will promise you. I will make love to you," he said softly, "but not until you come to me, begging for it."

"Never," she hissed, glaring up at him. "You'll never live to see me begging you for sex, ever."

Instead of backing off he only laughed. "And one more thing. You won't get my promise that I won't kiss you but you can rest assured that I will never make love to you unless you come to me first. And trust me, you will."

"You arrogant ass. Do you think you're irresistible?" She was breathing hard now, she was that angry.

"I know I am," the conceited pig replied, so full of himself it made her want to deliver a swift kick to his shin.

"We'll just see about that."

And that was where their conversation ended because she turned on her heel and stalked off, the sound of his laughter ringing in her ears.

He'd laughed at her then but tonight, their wedding night, Lani was going to have the last laugh. Tonight they would see who could resist who.

After the wedding Ridge had flown them to Hawaii in his private jet. That night in the bridal suite of Grand MoloKa'i Hotel Lani made preparations to be as alluring and seductive as she possibly could. Luckily, the bridal suite had two bedrooms so, quickly claiming one of them then making sure to close the door firmly behind her, she had no problem in doing her thing in private. She'd always been the casual type, usually a make-up free, pajama-wearing kind of girl. Tonight, though, she would go all out. She would make Ridge want her so bad his teeth would hurt.

After a leisurely bath in the Jacuzzi tub Lani patted herself dry then sat on the padded bench where she spent a good six or seven minutes massaging rose-scented body oil into her skin. She finished by spritzing her favorite perfume, Estee Lauder Pleasures, behind her ears and along the column of her neck. Now it was time to dress.

Still nude, she left the bathroom and walked into the bedroom, confident that Ridge would stick to his own quarters. He might be a cad but she could tell he was not the sort to invade someone else's privacy. At least he had that one good quality.

In the bedroom she went straight to the chest of drawers and pulled out her piece-de-resistance, a crimson G-string with black lace along the waistband, a garment so tiny she had to wonder why they charged so much for such a tiny scrap of cloth. Then she smiled to herself. It wasn't the size, of course, but the impact and with this bit of garment she planned to have the maximum impact possible.

She stepped into the G-string and pulled it up her legs and over her buttocks, making sure the tiny bow settled right at the top of the valley between the cheeks. Turning, she glanced back into the mirror. Perfect.

Next, she went back to her stash of sexy secrets and pulled out a diaphanous red teddy that left her shoulders and arms exposed. Dressing carefully in the see-through lingerie, she made sure the neckline fell just right, leaving much of her skin bare to the gaze. Not that her neckline was what would hold Ridge's attention. The sexy top was near-transparent, leaving hardly anything to the imagination. If Ridge was like any other red-blooded man his eyes would be glued to the curves of her breasts and the rose buds of her nipples as they winked at him from behind their gauzy veil.

Last, she slid her feet into high heeled sandals, transparent like glass to give him a nice view of her painted toenails, and with a feathery red puff on top of each, giving the footwear a naughty flair.

Ready now, she glanced in the mirror again and smiled, satisfied that she would have the effect she was aiming for. When he saw her Ridge Kent was sure to stand at attention – in more ways than one.

Biting her lips to keep from grinning, Lani opened her bathroom door and peeked out. Good. Ridge was in the suite living room, lounging on the sofa, a glass of wine in hand. There was another glass on the table in front of him, like he'd been waiting for her to emerge from her room. He was sitting there, staring off into space, and he looked lonely. Well, he wouldn't be lonely for long. Like it or not, he was about to be entertained by Lani Donatelli.

When she stepped into the living room Ridge's head jerked up, his eyes widening instantly as he took in her garb. She saw him suck in his breath and then he sat forward and rested his glass on the coffee table. His gaze fixed on her, Ridge's stare was unwavering but still he said nothing. Maybe he'd been shocked into silence.

Encouraged by his reaction, Lani's lips curved in a smile and, doing her best Marilyn Munroe impression, she pouted her lips then sauntered toward the man who sat watching her, obviously stunned.

She came to a halt just a few feet in front of him and, hand on her right hip, she struck a provocative pose. And just to make things that much sexier she glanced at the extra glass of wine and pointed with her ruby-red lips. "Is that for me?"

Ridge blinked. Then he cleared his throat. "Er, yes. It's...for you."

"Thank you," she purred and then, taking her own sweet time, she sashayed her way around the table, making sure he had enough time to check her out – the way the high heels elongated her legs, the peaks of her breasts beneath the sheer fabric and the red bow adorning the top of her behind.

When Ridge slid back in his chair, eyes glued to her gossamer-covered torso, he swallowed. Hard. It was no secret she was having just the kind of effect she was hoping for.

And so she moved in for the kill. With a beguiling smile she slid onto the seat beside him and reached for the glass of wine, not shielding her barely covered body from his gaze. She'd never been a shy girl and she certainly wasn't going to be shy now, not tonight when she wanted to torture Ridge until he begged for mercy.

So he thought she would be the one to come knocking, begging for sex? She bet, after the eyeful she'd just given him, he wasn't quite so cocky. No, she wouldn't be doing the begging. He was the one who would come knocking at her door and her answer would be a big, fat no. She could hardly wait to pay him back for that arrogant declaration he'd made.

Glass in hand, she settled back into the sofa and, still watching him, took a slow sip, savoring the velvety liquid on her tongue. Sitting so close she could feel the warmth of his arm that was almost touching hers, she turned so their faces were mere inches apart.

"Is there anything you would like to ask me?" she whispered, knowing that he understood exactly what she was talking about.

Instead of admitting defeat Ridge scowled back at her. "No," he muttered. "Nothing at all."

Lani smiled and nodded, not at all surprised. He was trying to play tough but not to worry. The night was still young and before it was gone she intended to bring him to his knees.

There was nothing left to say but, let the games begin.

***

What the bloody hell kind of game was Lani playing? The woman was mad.

Sultry and sexy as a siren she'd come out of her bedroom dressed in nothing but a G-string and God knew what that thing was she'd thrown over it. She might as well have walked out stark naked. He could see everything. Her body was covered in what looked like a red haze. There was no way he could call that clothes. He was seeing right through the damn thing.

And what a view. Damn, she was gorgeous. Small, pert breasts with red rubies at the tips, a taut torso that rivaled any model's and those legs, looking so long and lean in elegant high-heeled sandals. If she'd been trying to get him all hot and bothered she'd done a hell of a job.

And she knew exactly what she was doing, the wicked little minx. The naughty glint in her dark eyes and the impish curve of her lips told it all. She'd come out here with plans to drive him crazy with want and, by God, it was working. If the rigid rod in his pants was anything to go by he was in big trouble.

Clearing his throat again, he shifted on the sofa and made to get up. "Uhm, give me a sec, will you?"

Eyes sparkling with mischief, the devilish diva leaned in even closer. "Leaving so soon?"

He wouldn't give her that satisfaction. "Not leaving," he said tersely. "I just need something from the bedroom." And before he let himself down and reached for her he got up and took the quick steps that took him far enough away where he could breathe again. Jesus, did she see the way she was making him sweat? And he didn't mean that in a figurative sense, either.

Her soft chuckle filling his ears, Ridge escaped to the bedroom and closed the door. He needed a few seconds – no, more like a few minutes – to get over the shock of this new Lani. It was like she'd transformed from serious scientist to sensual siren, all in one day.

Now if this were a real marriage it wouldn't be a problem but like a fool he'd gone and made a promise that was backfiring big time. Why the blue blazes had he made that big boast that he wouldn't touch her? Letting out a frustrated sigh he heaved away from the door, his mind going helter skelter as he thrashed around for a plan of his own. Counter attack – that was the best course of action. But how?

Glancing around the room, his eyes fell on the robe he'd dropped on top of the bed after his shower. That was it. She'd come out showing off her body. Well, two could play that game.

Shedding the loose cotton pants and T-shirt he'd been wearing, he slid into the robe, letting it fall open to show his boxer shorts. Okay, so his robe made of white terry cloth wasn't sexy like hers but it would have to do.

The boxer shorts, though... He put a finger to his chin as he thought about it. No, too practical. He had to wear something else. There was one thing he could draw for, one of the wedding presents Ryder had given him, a gift he would not have expected from the serious, steady one.

"Thank you, Ryder," he muttered and strode over to his suitcase which he hadn't even bothered to unpack. He dug around in the inner compartment until he felt the silk fabric. When he pulled it out his face broke into a wide grin. It was slick, it was smooth and it was in tiger print. A G-string of his own.

Who was going to be sexy now? Quickly, Ridge stepped out of his boxers and slid the G-string up his legs and over his butt cheeks. It wasn't too comfortable but if that was what it would take to get back at little Miss Lani then he would do it. As if he hadn't wanted her enough before, she'd come out in all her glory and made him want her even more. Now it was her turn to want him.

And he would make her want him, lust after him, and then he would turn her down cold.

Satisfied with his plan, Ridge sucked in his stomach and flexed his shoulder muscles. So he wasn't Dwayne Johnson AKA The Rock, but he worked out and his body was in pretty good shape. If Lani was like the women who'd come his way she would be all over him when he walked back into the living room.

And so, his confidence back, Ridge strolled into the living room, ready to wow a wayward temptress.

When he stepped into the room Lani was still sitting on the sofa where he'd left her. As he approached, she looked up and her brows rose in surprise. And then she spoiled it with an amused grin. "Oh, my God. Are you trying to turn me on?"

And then she laughed. And if he'd had any thought of playing sexy stud that evening, she nipped that right in the bud. Talk about a buzzkill.

"No," he mumbled. "Of course not." And then as casually as he could he pulled the robe shut.

"No, you were. You were trying to tempt me," she said, insisting on rubbing his face in the pile of embarrassment dumped on the floor. "You were wearing a G-string. Oh, my God."

That did it. Scowling, Ridge turned right around and went back the way he'd come, slamming the door behind him.

Lani Donatelli knew exactly how to rub him the wrong way. She'd won this first round but she'd better come good next time.

Because there would definitely be a next time and when it came he would be more than ready.

CHAPTER FIVE

"Some more coffee, madam?"

Lani looked up as the server leaned down, coffee pot in hand.

"Oh, no, thank you. I'm fine." Smiling, she shook her head and watched as the colorfully clothed man gave her a polite bow then drew away.

She looked over at Ridge sitting across from her at the breakfast table. "The service here is superb," she said. "They give you no chance to need a single thing."

"That's why I chose this hotel for our honeymoon," he said and then as if remembering that he was supposed to be there on honeymoon, he frowned. He didn't say anything further, though, probably because he was still embarrassed about the events of the night before.

"Good choice," she said as she reached for the snow-white napkin and dabbed at her lips. Feeling a little guilty at how she'd behaved, today she was trying her best to be nice. The night before she'd wanted to burst his bubble of arrogance but she hadn't intended to devastate him. He was a fellow human being, after all.

The truth was, although she'd made a big show of laughing he'd actually shocked her when he came out in his super skimpy underwear... and he'd turned her on. She would never admit it, not to him anyway, but when she'd seen his body, all muscle and brawn, her mouth had literally gone dry.

Ridge was a big man. That was no secret but seeing him with no clothes on... wow. The man's abs looked solid as rock and the fine hairs on his torso only added to his ultra-masculine aura.

On seeing him like that Lani's imagination went wild. She could just imagine what it would be like to have his arms wrapped around her, crushing her to the solid wall of his chest. What normal girl wouldn't melt in the arms of a man like that? She knew she'd be practically swooning in his embrace...if she ever let him get close. She'd have to tread very carefully around this man because it would be too easy to get lost in the feel of him, the smell of him, the taste of him when she ran her tongue up...

"Ready to roll?"

Lani jumped, Ridge's words shattering her fantasy world. "Are we going somewhere?" she asked, more than willing to just go back to the suite and vegetate. It had been hectic, getting ready for a wedding in two weeks, so she would be happy to just chill and catch up on her sleep.

"I thought you'd like to explore the island," Ridge said. "Have you ever been to Halawa Valley Lookout or Kauleonanahoa?"

"Nope. This is my first visit to Hawaii." She shrugged. "I've been busy with my research. Who's had time for vacations?" And then she realized something. "Do you know, this is the first vacation I've had since I started working at the lab?" She smiled. "I wonder how the guys are doing without me?"

"I'm sure they're doing just fine. I hope you're not one of those workaholics who can't leave the office behind." Ridge gave her a sardonic grin.

"No way," Lani assured him. "When it's time for fun I can let my hair down." Then she chuckled. "Not that I have much to do it with." She'd let her hair grow a little longer for the wedding, skipping her regular appointment for a cut, and it was still in the softly curled style the hairdresser had given her for the special occasion. As soon as got back she was going to get her regular cut, though. That was much more practical when you had to do twelve-hour days and even weekends sometimes. With a schedule like that, who had time to titivate?

"Well, come on, then." Ridge said, hopping up from his chair and coming around to help her with hers. "Let's catch that island tour they're doing this morning. That's got to be better than being stuck in a hotel room all day."

Lani shook her head but she got up and took his hand. Hotel room, he called it. The bridal suite was twice as big as her condo apartment and, not to mention, it was super-luxurious. She had absolutely no problem being stuck in a place like that. But if a tour was what Ridge wanted then that was what she would do. At least she wouldn't have to worry about him coming up with mischievous plots while they were out in public.

In the end Lani didn't regret her decision to go. Halawa Valley was exquisite in its beauty, with views of the two hundred and fifty foot Moa'ula Falls and the even taller Hipuapua Falls. From the lookout above the valley they could take in the landscape of grassy plains and craggy mountains with lush flora climbing up to the falls and lazy rivers running into the deep blue ocean.

From there they headed for Kauleonanahoa. Lani had the hardest time pronouncing it. "What the heck does it mean, anyway?" she asked, finally giving up on her attempt to say the word. "Maybe if I know the meaning I can come up with a suitable abbreviation."

Ridge gave her a crooked smile as he looked down at her from his way taller than six-foot height. "You're sure you want to know?"

"Yeah. Why not?"

"Because it's referring to the phallic stone of Moloka'i. The word means 'the penis of Nanahoa.'"

Surprised, Lani raised her eyebrows. "Really?"

Ridge nodded. "It's a six-foot high symbol of fertility." Then he chuckled. "You never know. It may give you some ideas."

"I doubt it."

Later when she saw the rock she had to admit it was a sight to behold. A naturally formed rock looking like that personal part of the male anatomy. Imagine that. And although Ridge would never hear it from her lips, the rock looked so like the real thing that it did give her some ideas, naughty ones which would best be kept to herself.

And it was a good thing she did, too, because that night when they got back to their suite Ridge looked like all that hiking and fresh air had made him raunchy as a ram. He wasn't making any unwanted moves on her – he was probably too much of a gentleman to overstep his boundaries – but he was restless as a three-year old, pacing back and forth in the living room until she feared he would wear a path in the carpet. Then when he tired of that he went out onto the balcony, flopped down onto the wicker sofa and propped his feet on the balcony railing but within minutes he was back inside again, pacing up and down until she had to throw him out.

When, almost an hour later, she went out onto the balcony and asked if he wanted to go down to dinner he shook his head. "Let's eat out here," he said. "Order room service. I'm not in the mood to mix and mingle tonight."

And so they dined in –Saimin, an Asian-style noodle soup, followed by chicken katsu and fried Mahimahi. They finished off with bowls of pineapple flavored shaved ice.

"Mmm, that was good," Lani said with a sigh. "I am so full." She gave a playful groan. "You're going to have to roll me into my room."

Instead of the laughter she'd expected for that funny comment she got a serious look from Ridge. He cleared his throat. "I've been meaning to talk to you about that," he said, his voice sounding strange in its brusqueness. "That's not your room anymore." And that was where he stopped, saying nothing more, like that terse statement was sufficient.

Lani waited but when nothing further seemed forthcoming she decided to speak. "What do you mean, that's not my room anymore?" she asked, frowning. And then her face cleared. "You're such a child. Do you mean to tell me you want us to switch rooms just because I picked the bigger one? Oh, please. Grow up, will you?" She was laughing now, laughing at him for being so petty.

"That's not what I meant," he said, and he wasn't laughing. "I meant that you're not going to be sleeping in that room anymore. Neither am I. You're going to be sleeping with me."

Lani's brows shot up then she folded her arms across her chest and glared back at Ridge. "Excuse me? Have you forgotten something? Just in case you did, let me remind you. We have an agreement."

"And that agreement stands," he responded, his tone cold. "I told you I would not make love to you, not unless you wanted me to. I intend to honor that agreement." Then he sat forward and the dark-eyed gaze he fixed on her was determined. "But I never said that would mean we were going to occupy separate spaces."

Lani gasped, shocked that he would put such a spin on things. "No, you never said that but of course I assumed-"

"You assumed wrong."

But Lani was not about to accept that. "So why didn't you stop me when I unpacked my stuff in that other room? Why am I hearing about this now?"

"Because," he said with a shrug, a casual gesture that belied the intensity of his gaze, "I changed my mind."

"You can't do that," she said in strident protest.

"Who says I can't?"

"Well..." For a moment she was stumped. "Well, you just can't."

"Sure I can," he said, seeming to become more adamant by the second. "And I will. Tonight you're sleeping in my bed." When she opened her mouth to repeat her protest he put up a hand to stop her. "I'm not going to touch you. I already told you that. You have absolutely no reason to fear for your," he smiled, "feminine virtue."

"Then why are you doing this?" she half cried, half wailed. "Does it make sense for us to torture ourselves?" As soon as the words left her lips Lani realized her mistake.

Immediately, Ridge picked up on her slip of the tongue, his eyes lighting up with an ah-ha look. "Torture ourselves?" he asked, looking way too pleased. "It would only be mutual torture if I wanted you...and you wanted me right back. So," he sat back in his chair and folded his arms, the smile on his lips widening, "are you saying that you want me?"

"Never," she hissed and hopped up from her chair. "I would never give you that satisfaction."

"Hmm." He loosened his arms and lifted his hand to rub his chin in an exaggerated gesture of thoughtfulness. "Maybe you should think about that. You might want to consider giving yourself the satisfaction."

"Ugh." With a a guttural explosion of frustration Lani whirled around and marched back into the suite and straight to her room. Yes, it was her room and she was not going to let Ridge Kent bully her out of it. She would lock the door if she had to.

And she would have, except that the stupid door didn't have a lock. She couldn't even resort to the option of propping a tilted chair behind the door. Outside of the sofa and two wicker armchairs there were only bar stools at the kitchen counter. For a place this posh you'd think they would have even one real chair. Darn.

And so when Ridge left the balcony and came – uninvited – into her room, it was to find her sitting on her bed, arms folded, still sulking. She'd had such a high opinion of him, thinking he would never invade her space. Well, not anymore. Her opinion of him just plummeted to an all-time low.

"Come on, Lani," he said, going over to the closet. "Stop pouting and help me pack up your stuff."

"Just what do you think you're doing?" She hopped up off the bed and went right over to the closet then stood in front of him, trying to block his view to her stuff. Of course, she was too short for that. The man towered over her which meant all he had to do was look straight ahead to see everything. Her presence was no hindrance whatsoever.

"I'm going to help you pack," he said as if he did that sort of thing everyday.

"No, you're not," she said and jammed her fists on her hips. "Not over my dead body."

"Okay," he said, "no problem. We don't have to do this over your dead body. We'll just do it over your live one." And he reached over her head and began pulling her clothes from the racks.

"Stop that," she shrieked and reached up to try and rip the garments from his hands but he frustrated her even more when he just held them up high, forcing her to jump and even then she couldn't get the darned things.

After jumping a couple of times and realizing it was hopeless she stopped and resorted to glowering at him. "Ugh, you beast," she snarled and then, not knowing what else to do, she stormed out of the room and onto the balcony. There she flung herself into the nearest chair and stared out into the night that had now fallen over the land.

It was a good hour before Lani made her way back into the suite. By then Ridge would have probably moved all her clothes over to his room. At this point she didn't even care. She just wanted to get this so-called honeymoon over and done with so she could get on with her life.

She went back to her bedroom and, as expected, it was bare. The man was determined she should move to his room, so she would. She didn't give a hoot. As long as he didn't touch her she didn't really care.

And then she smiled, realizing that things might actually work in her favor. She'd wanted to torture him, hadn't she? What better way than to put temptation right under his nose? Laughing to herself she left her old room and, not even bothering to knock, she walked into her new place of abode.

And there he was, lying on top of the bed, hair damp, his hands clasped behind his head. He was watching her expectantly. "Took you long enough." He didn't sound angry, only amused.

She walked over to the chest of drawers. "I had a lot to think about." She opened the top drawer and, as she guessed, he'd already put some of her stuff there. Her intimates. He'd had his fingers on her undies but if that gave him joy she couldn't care less. As long as he didn't think that gave him the right to touch her.

But, unfortunately for him, in the next few minutes he would get an unexpected show and boy, would he be tempted to touch. Too bad for him she wouldn't let him.

Tonight she grabbed bikini panties and a black lace teddy, not as skimpy as the one she'd worn the night before but good enough, and then she was off to the shower. His shower. Now theirs. She gritted her teeth at the thought.

She took her time, savoring the warm spray massaging her back and shoulders, and then she donned her new costume and checked herself in the full-length mirror. The midnight-black silk teddy was in stark contrast to her pale skin, pale from all the hours locked away in the research lab, but the shimmering black material was a perfect match for the shiny-black shade of her damply curling hair.

When she went back into the room Ridge had pulled the covers down and he was still lying on his back but now he didn't seem quite as relaxed as before. His arms folded across his chest, he was watching her enter the room, his eyes following her as she walked around the foot of the bed and then to the other side. His gaze was roaming over her body, taking her in from head to toe, practically burning into her skin.

When she got into the bed she didn't slide in with her back toward the middle as she normally would. No, this time she climbed on, making sure to tilt forward, giving her now very tense 'husband' an unobstructed view of her breasts falling against the fabric of her skimpy top.

His sharp intake of breath told her all she needed to know. Ridge Kent was pretending to be unaffected by her display but he wanted her real bad and the evidence was there right in front of her eyes.

Why else would his shoulder muscles flex as he clenched his hands around his elbows? Why else would his nostrils be flaring like that?

Why else, for goodness gracious sake, would he have a rapidly rising mound tenting the front of his pants?

And then just as she settled onto the pillow beside him Ridge gave a groan fraught with frustration then rolled away from her and got out of the bed. Without warning he walked away into the bathroom and she didn't hear anything else until the shower started.

Ridge was mad all right, but he'd asked for it. She chuckled as she remembered his reaction. "Be careful what you wish for," she murmured. "You might just get it." ***

It was early, barely six o'clock in the morning but Ridge was up and jogging on the cool sand of Papohaku Beach. If he'd spent another minute with Lani's warm, sweet-smelling body curled up against his he'd have gone mad.

That is, if he wasn't already. Who but a mad man would put his own damn self in a prison of torment, living with a desirable woman but not able to touch her, then worsen the torment by bringing her into his own bed? No, you had to be crazy to willingly put yourself in such a fix. And that was exactly what he was. Crazy.

Exhausted from pushing himself hard, Ridge jogged over to a rock jutting out of the sand and dropped down onto it. Still panting, he raised his head to stare at the low-lying clouds tinted red and gold by the emerging rays of the early morning sun, a picture so serene it was in direct contrast to the turmoil that raged within him. Last night he'd had to resort to a quick, cold shower just to get his body to calm down. After enduring a sleepless night listening to Lani's gentle breathing, conscious of her lying next to him, he'd had to leave her there and escape to the beach just so he could breathe again. And think.

And as he sat there on his rock, a solitary figure on the stretch of beach, Ridge came to a decision. None of this made any sense. The only way he'd be able to preserve his sanity was to put a stop to it.

When he got back to the suite he didn't even enter the bedroom. That kind of sweet torture, he could do without. For the next couple of hours while Lani slept he hung out in the living room watching reruns of classic comedy shows. He'd always been a fan of 'The Honeymooners' and 'I Love Lucy' and he welcomed the distraction.

Contrary to what he'd expected, though, after sitting through four episodes of comedy he was in no better mood than when he'd left early that morning. In fact, when Lani finally emerged from the bedroom, scantily clad and making him even more aware of her as she spread her arms in a languorous stretch, his mood got even worse.

He didn't mince words. "We're leaving," he said. "Today. You can start packing right now."

Lani froze mid-stretch then she lowered her arms to her sides and frowned. "So soon? I thought this was supposed to be a week-long honeymoon."

"I've had enough," he said, his voice terse. "It's time for me to get back to the real world."

"Well." That was all she said – no protest, no nothing – then she shrugged and headed back into the bedroom.

Ridge grimaced then let out the breath he'd been holding. The truth was, he'd expected a fight, maybe even an all-out war. The last thing he'd expected was for her to accept his sudden change of plans without demur.

But he was thankful. He was looking forward to getting back to Houston where he could lose himself in the day-to-day problems of work. With all that distraction maybe he would be able to deal with his dilemma. This romantic setting was definitely not working in his favor.

But, back in Houston Ridge soon found out that losing himself in work was not going to be the answer. Each night he still had to come home to face a bride, now a wife of over one week, who proved a constant distraction. And as if that weren't bad enough she was a constant cause for vexation. The woman would not listen to him.

As soon as they'd arrived back in Texas the woman decided she was going back to work the very next day.

"You already told your staff you'd be away this week," Ridge told her. "Why don't you just stay in and relax?"

Instead of seeing reason Lani had a ready response. "So you rush us back here so you can get back to work but I should sit in the house for the rest of the week, bored out of my mind? Nothing doing."

"You were the one who complained that you hadn't had a vacation since taking that job."

"I didn't complain," she retorted. "I merely stated a fact. But that's beside the point. The important thing is, we're back in Houston and I'm certainly not going to waste time sitting in your big old house, twiddling my thumbs when I could be getting some good work done."

"Just like I thought," Ridge said, his lips twisting in annoyance. "You're nothing but a workaholic."

"Says the man who cut our honeymoon short so he could get back to work." Her laughter told him she was not intimidated by him, not in the least.

And that was the pity because if she would only listen to him then she wouldn't keep doing things that pissed him off... except that she seemed to take pride in her ability to do just that.

They'd been living together a little over a week in this ranch house – the one she'd called his big old house – when he came home much later than usual, almost nine o'clock that night, to find that she wasn't there. It was the first time he'd come home and she hadn't been there.

Frowning, he threw his jacket onto the sofa and fished his cell phone out of his back pocket. He dialed her number. It went straight to voicemail. Not what he wanted to hear.

A twinge of worry made his frown deepen but he sucked it in. Maybe he was overreacting. Lani was probably working late. He would give her another ten minutes and if she didn't get home by then he would try her phone again.

The second the clock told him the time had passed he tried her number. Voicemail again. What the heck? What reason would she have for turning off her cell phone? If she had to be in a meeting all she had to do was put the darned phone on silent mode. At least then she would know he was trying to reach her. With a growl of frustration Ridge went and retrieved his wallet from his jacket pocket then dug around until he found her card. Not caring what meeting or experiment he might be disturbing he dialed the number to the research lab. No friggin' answer.

By this time, the twinge of worry had turned into a knot inside his gut. What if something had happened to Lani? He didn't want to make a big thing out of what was probably nothing but after nine o'clock at night was not the time for a man to be wondering where his wife was. And rather than just sitting there, wondering, he decided to make a move. If he couldn't get Lani on the phone then he would have to go to her office.

Ridge shoved his phone into his trouser pocket, grabbed his keys and was just heading for the door when he heard a car pull into the driveway. Lani was home. Finally. A wave of relief washed over him but within seconds it had morphed into anger. She'd better have a damn good reason for coming home at this hour.

When the front door opened he was standing there in the foyer, waiting for her. "Why didn't you call me?"

Lani jumped but as her gaze fell on him she smiled. "You startled me," she said, coming in and closing the door behind her. "That's not nice."

"And it's not nice to have your husband at home wondering where the hell you are."

At his biting retort Lani frowned. "I'm a grown woman. I can come home whenever I want to." She dropped her bag onto the hallway table and made as if to walk away but he stepped in front of her, bringing her to a sharp halt.

"You may be a grown woman," he said, his tone cold, "but you're a married woman now. You've got a husband to answer to, and don't you forget it."

"Well, excuse me." Her words dripping with sarcasm, she glared at him. "Just in case you missed the memo, this is the twenty-first century. Being married to you doesn't mean you own me." She folded her arms across her lab coat covered frame, looking ready for a fight.

Pissed that instead of apologizing she was being combative he hit back just as hard. "I may not own you but as long as you're my wife you check in with me or-"

"Or what?" Now she'd loosened her crossed arms and had them curved outward, looking like a teenage street thug fixing for a beat-down. He would have laughed if he weren't so mad.

"Will you shut up and listen to what I have to say? All I was saying was you-"

"No, I will not shut up. No man's going to tell me to shut up, husband or no husband."

"Lani, I'm warning you. Be quiet or else-"

"Oh, so you're threatening me now? You think because I agreed to marry you I signed over the rights to my freedom? Well, you got it wrong, buster." And then she did that jerky thing with her neck that feisty women do when they're telling you off.

"You asked for this," he muttered and before she could make another move he'd reached out, clamped his hands on her shoulders and hauled her toward him.

Lani gasped but it was too late. She'd had her chance to shut up. Now it was up to Ridge to do it for her.

Pulling her smack against him he reached his hand up to cup the back of her head then he tilted her so she was perfectly positioned for his kiss. As he lowered his lips she closed her eyes tight but her mouth softened and he could tell she wanted this. Her body would not lie.

Taking his cue from her response Ridge covered her lips with his own, exacting her silence with his kiss, not letting up until her body melted against him, her will yielding to his.

When he finally withdrew and gazed down at her face her eyes were still closed. Slowly he released her so she could again stand on her own.

It was only then that she opened her eyes. Her wide-eyed gaze never leaving his face, she drew in a shaky breath. "I thought you said you wouldn't force me...to do anything like that." Her voice had a breathless tone that told him she'd been shaken by his move.

"No," he said, watching the erratic beat of the pulse at the base of her neck. "I said I'd never make love to you, not if you didn't want me to." He gave her a crooked smile. "Now kissing, that's another matter altogether."

Her answer was a scalding look which made Ridge laugh as he stepped away, giving her the freedom to move.

As she stepped past him he gave in to the temptation for one last jab. "I think I've found the perfect punishment for you so you'd better stay in line."

He wasn't surprised when, instead of answering, she flounced off. He only chuckled. Then, as he watched her head off to her room, he muttered under his breath, "Yeah, you'd better watch it, sister. I'd be only too happy to punish you every day of the week."

CHAPTER SIX

Damn, the man could kiss.

Over a dozen hours had passed since Ridge grabbed her and kissed the anger out of her but Lani could still feel his muscled body stamped on hers and his lips taking full control. She had a test tube in one hand and a pipette in the other but her eyes were staring blankly out the window as she relived those super-hot blazing seconds he'd held her in his arms.

She'd been dead tired when she'd arrived home last night and then he'd gone and annoyed her with his reprimand. And then, in the midst of it all, he lit a fire inside her which raged all night, making her toss and turn into the wee hours of morning. His kiss had awakened a thirst inside, one which could not be quenched until she'd had more of him. All of him. She knew that now.

"I'm beginning to worry about you."

At the sound of Chris's voice, Lani turned. "What's there to worry about?"

"You've been standing there, staring out the window for at least five minutes. You on drugs or something?"

"What kind of question is that to ask your boss?" Lani burst out laughing. "You're something else, do you know that?"

Chris laughed back. "No, I'm just a guy who's glad he's got a boss with a sense of humor." Then his face sobered. "But seriously, though, are you okay? Your mind's still on that stack of bills that came in before your vacation?"

"No, that's all taken care of." This time her smile was full of relief. "The lease payments are up-to-date. In fact, where the bills are concerned, I'd say we're good till at least the end of the year."

"Holy..." Chris gazed at her in wonder. "Did one of those big drug companies finally cave and give you the money? What did you do? Hold a gun to somebody's head?"

"Chris, Chris," she shook her head, "you have such a low opinion of me. Could you even see me doing something like that?"

He gave her a look which was practically a roll of the eyes. "I'm sure you don't want me to answer that."

"Well, don't." She gave him a wry grin. "If you want to keep your job you'd better be nice."

"Yes, boss." With a grin and a salute he turned and headed back to his side of the lab, leaving Lani to daydream in peace.

And daydream she did, practically the whole morning and part of the afternoon. She wanted Ridge but after the big deal she'd made about him not touching her, how could she admit to the attraction?

After another hour of being less than her productive self Lani gave up. "I'm heading out," she told Chris. "You're good until Minerva gets here?"

"Sure. You go on home. You're looking kind of tired."

"I am?" Was her sleepless night that obvious? "Well, I guess I'd better go, then."

"Yeah, go get some sleep, boss."

Lani left but she had no plans to get any sleep. She was too revved up for that. That evening she decided to try her hand at the wife thing and spent a couple of hours in the kitchen fixing a meal of meatloaf, mashed potatoes and corn on the cob. Cooking had never been her strong point but she felt chastened enough to want to show Ridge she was making an effort. She really should have called him when she realized she would be home much later than usual. She knew she was at fault but at the time it hadn't seemed like a big deal, especially since they'd spent the past week barely seeing each other, each lost in their own world of work. It had actually crossed her mind that he might not even notice she wasn't home yet.

Wrong assumption. Based on his reaction Ridge had noticed, and in a big way, and the fact that her cell phone battery had died hadn't helped matters one bit. She should have thought of that, too. Damn her for being so used to living on her own. She really had to remember that she was living with someone now, someone who might wonder why she hadn't come home.

But that was all water under the bridge now and all she could do was show Ridge that she was sorry. She just hoped a hot home-cooked meal would do the trick.

Lani set the table and even went as far as to light the scented candles. Then, just as the sun began to set, she took her bath and dressed in a simple emerald-green shift and strappy sandals. She didn't own many dresses since she was far more comfortable in cargo pants or jeans so, if Ridge knew anything about her, he would know he was a lucky man tonight. She'd gone all out, just for him.

Just as she walked back into the dining room she heard his car pull up. Perfect timing. She went into the kitchen and began sliding the trays from the oven. The aroma of the savoring meat pie filled the kitchen and she ladled the food onto the dinner plates, proud of her handiwork. She was smiling to herself when she heard him call out.

"Something smells good. Lani, is that you?"

When his head popped around the kitchen door, his brows elevated in surprise, she laughed. "Who did you think it was? Your fairy godmother?"

"It might as well be," he said, stepping into the kitchen. "I can't believe you made dinner. I didn't know you could cook."

"Don't sing my praises just yet," she warned. "Wait until you take a bite. I just hope I don't send us both to the ER tonight."

He laughed. "I'm sure you won't. It smells so good my mouth is watering already."

And Lani's mouth was watering, too, but it wasn't for meatloaf and potatoes. It was for the handsome hunk who stood before her, six o'clock shadow on his jaw, tie gone and stark-white collar open to give her a peek at the top of his broad chest. What would it feel like to run her tongue over the smooth silk of that skin?

Lani shook her head. She was thinking dangerous thoughts and she didn't need to go there. Not now, not yet. "Go take a quick shower," she said, trying to defuse the tension that was knotting in her stomach. "By the time you're done I'll have dinner on the table."

Ridge nodded. "You don't have to tell me twice." And in a flash he was gone, his footsteps sounding in the hallway as he headed for his bedroom.

"Wow," Lani whispered to herself. "He must be real hungry." At least she could hope so. Maybe that was why he hadn't even noticed the change in her attire. Didn't she look different?

Fifteen minutes later Ridge walked back into the living room, looking fresh and frustratingly handsome in ink-black trousers and matching black shirt. He walked right up to Lani as she sat at the table waiting for him and surprised her with a kiss on the cheek.

"That color suits you," he said. "You look stunning."

Lani didn't know which surprised her more - his kiss or his compliment. Her face broke into a smile. So he had noticed.

Ridge sat at the place she'd set for him across from her but then, like he could read her mind, like he could tell she was wanting him tonight, he got up and shifted his plate and utensils to the place right beside hers. "You're too beautiful," he said, his voice slightly hoarse, "for me to stay far away from you."

Lani raised her eyebrows. Hello? Where had that come from? She wasn't complaining, though, so she just smiled and said nothing.

After that Lani and Ridge enjoyed their meal which, to Lani's surprise, tasted pretty good if she should say so herself. She had to admit, too, that she enjoyed her conversation with Ridge, the first real one they'd had since getting married. Who could have known that Ridge Kent had a complex personality? Ever since they'd met at that first board meeting she'd seen him as a wise-cracking troublemaker who was only too happy to shove his opinion down other people's throats.

Now, though, he was opening himself up to her, showing her a whole new side to his personality.

"We owe it to our children and grandchildren," he was saying, "to do all we can to protect and preserve the environment. I feel strongly about this and that's the reason why I support research that will help us find viable energy alternatives."

Lani tilted her head, curious. "Seriously? But you're in the oil business. How do you reconcile the two?"

He shook his head. "Being in the oil industry doesn't stop me from being concerned. Right now I satisfy the community's energy needs but I also recognize that we need to find alternatives. And trust me," he smiled, "as we transition to those alternatives I'll be the first to jump on board. Where the business goes, I go."

She smiled back. "Spoken like a true capitalist."

He chuckled. "Did you expect anything less?"

After that their conversation moved to her research and the progress she was making in sourcing plant supplies for her experiments and trials. "Thanks to you," Lani said, "I don't have to be distracted by mundane matters like leases and bills. It's such a relief to be able to focus on what matters." She gave a soft sigh of contentment. "We've made quite a bit of progress and right now we're just waiting for a shipment from South America. Once that arrives we'll be able to complete phase one of the study."

"Sounds good," Ridge said. "I'm glad I was able to help."

And then Lani remembered. She was grateful for his help, of course, but it had come at a price. She'd had to leave her apartment and move into his house, sacrificing her freedom so she could get the funding she so desperately needed.

And so Lani was torn. On the one hand she recognized that if Ridge hadn't come to the rescue the landlord would have probably locked them out of the building by now. On the other hand, she was more than a little peeved. Ridge could have given her that money, easy. Why did he have to tack a condition onto it?

And so as he smiled at her she smiled back but her mind was ticking away, busy contemplating her next step. She'd started the evening with all kinds of good thoughts about Ridge. She'd wanted to show him she could be nice. More than that, though, she'd wanted to tempt him just a little, to see if she could get him to kiss her again. She'd tasted his kiss, not once but twice, and she wanted more.

But how could she divorce her desire from her displeasure? He'd blackmailed her, after all.

"You're still with me?"

Lani blinked and turned her gaze to Ridge who was watching her with interest.

"You looked like you had the weight of the world on your shoulders," he said. "What's up? Got something on your mind?"

Ignoring all the reasons why she shouldn't, Lani decided to be bold. She would go for what she wanted and be damned with discretion. Slowly, deliberately, she laid her napkin on the table then reached out and lifted her glass to take a fortifying sip of wine. Then she turned to face her friendly foe, deciding on a full frontal attack.

"I want to kiss you," she said, abandoning coyness and getting straight to the point. And she might be mad that he'd forced her into this situation but that didn't mean she didn't want him. She'd thought she could ignore him for a year but his kiss taught her otherwise. Now she would take her pleasure and deal with her vexation later.

"I'm all yours," Ridge said and made as if to get up but she dropped her hands on his shoulders, preventing him from moving.

Cupping his face in her hands she bent her head to rest her lips against his, reveling in the warmth of his mouth against hers. Then she pressed harder, forcing him to yield to her, allowing her entry. As he groaned and opened to her she took full control of the kiss, holding his face captive as she stood over him, tasting him, devouring him to her heart's content.

When she finally pulled away Ridge gazed up at her, his eyes all but glazed over. "God, you taste so good," he groaned and licked his lips like he meant it.

Instead of answering, Lani turned and sat on Ridge's lap and when she felt his hardness pressing up into her she smiled. Emboldened by this obvious sign of his ardor she reached her hand up to cup the back of his head then she pulled his face down toward hers and captured his lips again, showing him with her kiss that she was in control. Maybe it was the mixture of passion and indignation that raged within her or maybe it was because she'd held it in too long but she put everything in that kiss so that when she released him he looked stunned.

Before he could recover she gave him another shock when she reached down and ripped his shirt open, popping buttons, sending them flying.

With his shirt wide open, his muscled chest exposed, she slid off his lap but only to get back on top of him, this time with her legs straddling his. Facing him, she had full access to his bare and beautiful body. Without hesitation she leaned forward to capture a turgid nipple between her teeth. She nibbled and nipped, punishing his sensitive bud till he sucked in his breath and clenched his eyes shut but when she began to lick and soothe him with her tongue he flung his head back and moaned.

He lifted his hands like he wanted to touch her, hold her, but Lani slapped them away. Ridge might be bigger than she was but as long as she kept him in his chair she could control whatever happened and she planned to keep things that way. She would keep him entertained. That way he would have no need to rise. As long as the only rising he was doing was in his pants she was a happy camper.

Moving swiftly before he had the chance to wonder what would happen next Lani loosened the bow at her right shoulder and let the top of the shift fall forward, exposing her lace-covered bosom. His eyes still closed, Ridge had no idea what was going on but it didn't matter because in one fluid movement Lani stood, her hands pulling the clasp at the front of her bra as she moved. Now, with her breasts free, she leaned over Ridge's upturn face and nudged her nipple between his lips, feeding him the puckered fruit, feeling a thrill run through her body as he started then tasted then sucked it in.

Now, with that sensitive bud between his lips, it was Lani's turn to moan. As he drew it in, teasing it with his tongue, nipping it with his teeth, massaging it with his lips, Lani closed her eyes then threw her head back and moaned. She arched her back, pressing into him, wanting more of the molten pleasure that flowed from his lips. And even as she moaned she felt the liquid warmth between her legs, testament to the effect Ridge was having on her.

Lani shifted, ready to feed the other bud to the ravenous rogue beneath her, when he lifted his hand to span her waist and lift her off him.

Eyes so intense they blazed, he got up and took her hand then jerked his chin toward the stairway. "Come on," he said, his voice raspy. "Let's do this right." He took her hand and turned, ready to finish what she'd started.

But it was too late. He'd broken the spell, dragged her out of her dreamy fantasy, the one where she'd orchestrated the whole thing. Now it was he who was calling the shots, just like he'd done when she'd turned to him in desperation. It was a jolt of reality that knocked the 'horny' right out of her. It was a reminder too stark, too strong for her to ignore. No matter how much she pretended, Ridge was the one in charge.

She pulled her hand from his grasp. "No." She shook her head. "That's it. I don't want to do this anymore."

Ridge pulled up short, his eyes filled with confusion. "What the hell? You started this."

"I know," she said, her voice terse. "And now I'm ending it." She stepped back, covering herself as she moved, then began to redo the bow that held the top of her dress in place.

"What? Why?" Ridge looked like he'd lost his bearings, like he didn't know if he was coming or going.

Too bad. The way she was feeling right now she had no sympathy for him. "I changed my mind," she told him with a shrug then moved away and began to stack the dirty dishes and bowls in the middle of the dining table.

"What the f-"

"Don't you dare." Lani fixed him with a glacial glare. "You don't need to sink so low."

"The hell I don't. What kind of friggin' game are you playing? You're trying to mess with my head?"

Lani shrugged then lifted the stack of china. "Let's just say," she murmured, "I can play games just as well as you." Not waiting for an answer she walked away, leaving him to stew in the sauce she'd served.

In the refuge of the kitchen she dropped the dishes into the sink and let out the breath she'd been holding. Thank goodness he hadn't followed her. He must be pissed as hell, with her leaving him high and dry like that.

But she couldn't help it. It was the memory of how she'd gotten here in the first place that had been her undoing. She just couldn't reconcile herself to the fact that he'd been all-powerful and she, so powerless.

And if the only way she could wield what little power she had was to withhold sex, then so be it.

The only sad thing about the whole affair was, in punishing him she was darned well punishing herself, too. And Lani had no idea how long she could hold out.

***

Not again. How could he have fallen for that again? Ridge slammed his palms down on the bathroom counter and glared at his reflection in the mirror.

He was a friggin' idiot, that was what he was. How could he let her play him like that? The woman was nothing but a little tease, a witch ready and willing to yank his chain. Drive him crazy. Torment him with want and then walk away. Damn!

Ridged slapped his hands down again but what he really wanted to do was drive his fists through the mirror. Pissed could not begin to describe what he was feeling.

That night, sleep was the furthest thing from his mind. He was so wound up it wasn't until the wee hours of morning that he finally drifted into a fitful sleep. At the sound of a car engine he woke with a start and that was when he realized it was morning and Lani was driving out, heading for work.

It was a grumpy and groggy Ridge who showed up at the office that morning. When he walked in he tried to fake a smile but his assistant could read him like an open book.

"You look terrible," Miss Poole said, giving him a stern once-over. "I would suggest you save the partying for the weekend."

Ridge just gave her a noncommittal grunt and kept walking until he'd entered his office and closed the door behind him. In the privacy of the room he relaxed his clenched teeth and gave way to a groan. He was exhausted and he was in the same bad mood Lani had put him in the night before. It was only because he had an important board meeting that afternoon that he'd even ventured out in public. He was in no condition to mix and mingle with anyone. Not today.

When Miss Poole buzzed to tell him it was time for his meeting he put on his game face and headed off to the conference room. It wasn't going to be easy but like any professional worth his salt he was going to have to push his personal problems to the distant corners of his mind and deal with the issues at hand.

It was a long four hours but Ridge made it to the end of the meeting. Unfortunately, it was not before he'd nearly chewed off the head of his CEO for making a costly blunder. For the most part he'd kept his anger under control but this wasn't one of those days when he was going to play nice.

When the meeting finally ended and he got up to go he could see the flash of relief that crossed the face of his second-in-command. Suddenly feeling guilty that he'd been so harsh, Ridge gave Jeff Bentley a curt nod. "We'll talk about this tomorrow," he said, his voice calm, the very opposite of what he'd been just minutes before. "We'll find a solution to this." With those words of reassurance he left the conference room and, not stopping, he left the office building and went straight to his Jaguar in his reserved parking spot. He was going home. There was something he needed to do and the sooner, the better.

Ridge was on his way to the house when he called Lani from his cell phone. Like he could have guessed, she was still at the lab, hard at work.

"Do you have a minute?" he asked. "Can you talk?"

There was a brief pause and when she spoke her voice was hesitant. After what she'd done to him she was probably expecting a shouting match. She would have a long wait for that one. "I'm sort of busy right now," she said. "I can only give you a couple of minutes."

"That's all I need," he said. "You got what you wanted. You won't have me around to bother you anymore."

He heard a soft gasp. "What are you talking about?" she asked.

"When you get home I won't be there," he said brusquely. "I'm moving out."

CHAPTER SEVEN

"Where's the flippin' travel pouch?"

Ridge was muttering to himself as he threw shirts, socks, underwear and trousers into his suitcase. By the time Lani got home from work he would be long gone and he couldn't have made a better decision. He would be far away from the little witch and he'd finally have peace.

After a few more frustrating minutes of searching he finally found the pouch he'd been looking for, tucked way to the back of the shelf in his closet. How that had gotten all the way back there, he couldn't tell. He'd probably been in one of his mad moods when he'd thrown it on top of the shelf. Now, with it plopped on top of his clothes, he could close his suitcase.

But just before he did there was one quick thing he wanted to do. He'd been wound so tight he'd been sweating buckets all day. He felt too sticky to go out like this. He glanced at the clock, checking to make sure he had enough time for a quick shower. He didn't want to be there when Lani got home but, knowing her, she wouldn't leave the lab until the sun had gone down.

Ridge had just shrugged out of his suit jacket and was reaching for his tie when he heard tires screeching down below. Frowning, he went over to the window. Shit. It was Lani. How had she gotten home so fast?

Looking like an angry swan with her white lab coat sailing behind her, the little woman hopped out of her car and tore up the driveway toward the front porch. Ridge heard when she flung the front door open and then her footsteps sounded on the stairs.

He shook his head. Why the heck had she bothered to come home? There was nothing she could say that would stop him from leaving.

He'd turned away from the window and was heading toward the bathroom as planned when his bedroom door burst open and Lani stood there, panting from her run. Her brows fell in a frown. "Where do you think you're going?" Then, like one of those wrestlers getting ready to rumble, she stood in the doorway, feet planted firmly apart, and folded her arms across her chest.

If Ridge weren't so dang tired of Lani and her games he would have laughed. Did she really think she could stop him? He turned to face her. "I'm leaving," he said, his voice stone cold. "You're driving me crazy. I'm getting out of here before I do something I regret."

That should have been enough to send any woman running, but not Lani. Instead of accepting his declaration and backing down in defeat, her face tightened. "You're not going anywhere."

Now Ridge did laugh. He couldn't help it. At his six-foot-four height and brawny build was he really being bullied by a woman a foot shorter than he was? "You gotta be kidding me," he said with a snort. "Who's going to stop me? You?" It was more a sneer of disdain than a question.

She didn't answer. At least not in words. Before he even realized what she was doing Lani was inside the room, standing right in front of him, her eyes flashing with fury. She caught him by surprise when her hand shot out and grabbed his tie. She yanked on it hard, almost breaking his neck. "I said you're not going anywhere."

Her hands shot up again but this time it was to grab fistfuls of his shirt then she was pushing against his chest, pushing with all her might, propelling him backwards toward the bed.

He could have stopped her. Easy. If he'd planted his feet firmly on the ground she couldn't have moved him an inch. But he couldn't believe it. The wee woman had him in shock. The little elf had actually gotten it into her head that she could boss him around.

Ridge was so bemused by his wife's fearless behavior that he didn't notice they'd reached the bed until she gave him a hearty shove in the chest, sending him tumbling backwards.

Before he could recover she was on top of him, straddling him even as she pulled at his tie, quickly loosening it and throwing it onto the floor. Then she was attacking his shirt, not pausing to loosen the buttons but ripping it open, sending buttons flying.

"Hey, that's the second shirt in two days." He didn't get the chance to say another word.

Lani clamped his face in her hands and lowered her lips to his then she was kissing him fiercely, so hungrily that she was like a woman gone wild. What made it worse, as she kissed him she was moaning like she really wanted this. Was she faking or was this real? God, she was driving him insane.

Panting now, wanting her like he'd never wanted her before, Ridge moved his hands up to capture her and lift her off him, breaking the kiss.

"Why did you do that?" she wailed, trying to get back on top of him.

But he wouldn't let her. He put up a hand to block her attempt to straddle his waist again. "I can't deal with this," he growled. "This damn teasing. You're driving me crazy."

To his surprise, Lani gave him a sly smile. "Who says I'm teasing?" she asked, her voice seductive and soft.

And at the sound of those words Ridge felt his heart stop and his hardness swell in his pants.

***

Lani wanted Ridge so bad her heart felt like it was ready to burst out of her chest. She'd always known she wanted him but her anger had always been that brake that kept her from giving him her all. But now, with the threat of him leaving for good, her anger had to take a back seat. There were other, more important things on the table right now, like holding on to this man, like fucking his brains out.

Yeah, she would go there. She'd turned bold, she'd turned forceful and she'd turned rude. Right now she didn't give a damn about decorum. She wanted Ridge here and now and she would have him even if it meant she would have to turn into a big, bad bitch to do it. She might be small in body but when it came to getting what she wanted she could be as big and bold as the best of them.

Grabbing his shirt as it flapped open, Lani heaved, letting Ridge know that she wanted him to rise.

Thank goodness he didn't resist. Eyes deep, dark and intense he raised up from how she'd had him lying flat on his back and when she kept tugging he got up off the bed.

Smiling with relief but glad he was letting her boss him around Lani hung on to his shirt and dragged Ridge off to the bathroom. For being such an obedient little boy – in this case, a really big, little boy – she would give him a special treat.

As soon as they were inside the bathroom Lani pushed Ridge back against the sink and dropped to her knees in front of him. She heard when he sucked in his breath but she pretended not to notice. Instead, she focused on the task at hand – getting Ridge good and naked.

Lani's hand flew to his belt and as she loosened it he groaned. She smiled. What did he think she was going to do to him? Moving quickly, she pulled the button at the top of his pants then reached for the zipper. Then, wanting to make him wait, wanting to watch him writhe, she began to pull it down, her movement tantalizingly slow. Like she knew he would, Ridge groaned again and now he'd reached behind him and was gripping the countertop so tight his knuckles were white.

Her smile deepening, Lani slid her hands inside Ridge's trousers, her palms gliding over the cotton-covered cheeks of his bottom then she pushed down, letting his trousers fall to the floor.

She let him step out of trousers, socks and shoes and shrug the shirt off his back and now he was standing in front of her with only one insignificant garment blocking her from her goal. Still on her knees,

Lani glanced up, an involuntary smile curling her lips when she saw the look on his face, a an endearing mix of desire, uncertainty and anticipation. She had him by the cojones now – figuratively speaking, of course – and if she played her cards right she would soon have him eating out of her hand.

Lani reached up and hooked her thumbs into the sides of Ridge's boxer shorts, ready to pull the underpants down and reveal him to her gaze but then she paused. Maybe she was a masochist, prolonging her torture, but she decided to wait just a little bit longer. He was ninety percent naked and she was fully clothed. How fair was that?

Lani got up from her knees, taking note of the soft hiss that escaped Ridge's lips as she moved away. She stifled her chuckle. The man had complained about her driving him mad. Pity he didn't know she was about to make things a whole lot worse.

Her gaze never leaving his face, Lani backed away, almost to the other end of the spacious bathroom, and it was from that vantage point that she began her striptease. Unbeknownst to Ridge, this evening she'd decided to be his very own private dancer.

She started with the coat, which she'd almost forgotten she was wearing. With a flourish she slid it off her back, twirled it around then dropped it on the floor. Next, she reached her hands up and slowly undid the buttons on her shirt, taking note that as her fingers went down the line, from button to button, Ridge's gaze was following every step of the way. Within seconds the shirt was dangling from her fingers and then it, too, was falling in a heap on the floor, leaving her top bare except for her bra.

By this time Ridge's eyes were glued on her, taking in every curve, looking like he was ready to devour her whole.

Lani stepped out of her loafers then dropped her hands to the waist of her slacks and began to undo the button there, making her moves sexy as sin. Shirt and slacks weren't exactly the best selection for a sexy striptease but she was making all the sultry moves to make up for that and if Ridge's reaction was anything to go by, it was working.

The big man didn't move as he watched her from across the room but his grip on the counter did not relax and when he swallowed his Adam's apple bobbed like a dinghy in distress. She was having an effect on him all right. A big one.

And Lani meant to keep it that way so, straightening her back to give him the full impact of her jutting breasts, she reached behind and pulled the clasp at her back then let the bra slide off her shoulders and down her arms, exposing her full breasts to his gaze. She was rewarded with his sharp intake of breath.

Not stopping there, she tilted forward and hooked her thumbs into the sides of her bikini underwear then slowly she pushed it down, off her bottom, down her legs and to the floor. When she straightened up and stepped out of the panties she looked over at Ridge again and this time there was no hiding his arousal. A sizable tent was jutting forward in his shorts, making his response no secret whatsoever.

Now, fully nude, the only thing covering her being the hair on top of her head, Lani moved toward Ridge, finally ready to put him out of his misery. She knew he wanted her but she also knew he was scared to make a move. It would be up to her to take things to the next level.

Her movements decisive, Lani went back to stand in front of Ridge, her eyes just level with the nipples on his chest, and although she was tempted to pause there, to give him pleasure by licking the stiff buds, she did not. There would be time enough for that later.

She dropped to her knees again but this time it was to hook her thumbs into the waistband of Ridge's shorts and push them down. Immediately, his manhood popped up, perplexed, purple and proud, as she pushed his shorts down past his knees and onto the floor. Slowly, she rose up from the floor, making her movements languid and sensual, and then she reached for his hand.

She couldn't help but smile at the look on his face, half wary, half disappointed. He was eager for more but she was the one calling the shots. He would just have to wait.

Lani led Ridge over to the Jacuzzi hot tub and as it filled with water she made him climb over and relax in its warmth. Climbing in beside him, she reached over to grab the bubble bath gel and the soft plastic mesh sponge. She lathered it then proceeded to stroke his chest, making him sigh and close his eyes then sink lower into the water. She didn't let him get away, though. Her hand slid down, following him, sliding under the bubbly water where she could continue her caress, but this time along the length of his strong legs.

Ridge was staring at her now and she knew what he wanted. It was time to reward him for letting her rule.

Her bold nature not letting her down, Lani moved the sponge up to his private area and proceeded to circle the heaviness that lay there.

Ridge gasped, his body shuddering as he clenched his eyes shut and flung his head back against the tub. Meanwhile, his arms spread wide against the back of the tub, he clutched the tiled lip, looking like he was clinging on for dear life.

But Lani did not stop there. She moved the sponge up until she was caressing that part of him that throbbed at each touch, and as she massaged she leaned forward to steal a kiss from the man who, by now, was breathing hard like he'd just finished the hundred-meter dash.

As she kissed him and Ridge kissed back hungrily she released him and moved her hands up so she could pinch his nipples, bringing them to a hardness that matched the one down below. Then she drew her lips away.

"Enough," she whispered. "Now it's your turn."

Ridge lifted his head and without hesitation he picked up the sponge and began to massage her collarbone and then her breasts, sending tingles running all through her body. Then, just like she'd done, he moved his hands lower, gliding the sponge over her body then down to that sweet spot between her legs and there he stayed, stroking her ever so softly with the sponge, stimulating the sensitive bud down there, sending sparks flying all throughout her body.

She was panting now, her breath coming in quick, shallow gasps as her eyelids grew heavy and fluttered closed.

The next thing she heard was a growl followed by a splash and as her eyes flew open she found herself lifted high in Ridge's arms. He hadn't said the word but it was the unmistakable sign that, like her, he'd had enough.

Ridge stepped out of the tub with her in his arms, grabbing a towel off the rack as he strode out of the bathroom. He threw the big bath towel on top of the bed then laid her gently, almost worshipfully, on top of it. Then, although he was still dripping wet, he leaned over her and proceeded to dab at her body with the ends of the towel, from her damp arms to her legs and then to her glistening breasts.

But then as his eyes slid down to the shadowy V between her legs he paused and drew in a deep breath. Then he licked his lips, his gaze hungry.

Lani held her breath. She didn't have long to wait. As she watched, near mesmerized, Ridge sat on the end of the towel beside her, right by her legs, then he lowered his face to her, so agonizingly slowly that she was tempted to reach out and grab his head. But when he got there it was worth the wait.

Ridge settled his lips right there, where he teased her with butterfly kisses that sent thrills rippling through her body. Then, to her delight, his tongue shot out and he was licking the drops of water from her skin, teasing her mercilessly, making her head fall back and her legs relax, leaving her open to his caress.

Ridge took full advantage of her acquiescence. Flattening his tongue, he licked her till she moaned out loud and this time she did reach for him, clutching his shoulders, pulling him into her, wanting even more.

He readily obliged, moving his tongue lower to taste her, exploring her so intimately that her face burned even as she reveled in his caress.

When he withdrew she sighed out loud, her body still singing with the tune he'd played on her. And now she wanted him even more.

She felt when Ridge climbed onto the bed beside her and then he was reaching for her, pulling her into his arms. When he pressed his lips to hers she gladly opened to him, kissing back eagerly, telling him with her response that she was ready.

She knew he got the message when he raised his body then pulled her beneath him. She sighed and relaxed, waiting for the crinkly sound of the condom packet as he ripped it open. It never came.

And now Ridge was positioning himself between her legs, readying himself to enter her.

Her eyes flew open. "Wait," she whispered, her hands still clinging to the solid muscles of his shoulders. "You forgot the condom."

Ridge froze. Then he looked down at her and when he did his face was perplexed. "Condom?" he said, his voice hoarse. "I don't have any."

She drew in her breath. Then she frowned. "Why don't you have any? You had no plans for making love?"

Ridge scowled right back. "You're my wife. I don't need a condom to make love to my wife."

"And what about babies?" He was so daft. It didn't matter that they both had medical reports saying they were clean. That wasn't the only thing to worry about.

"Godammit," he grated. "Don't tell me you're going to make me stop now."

"But we can't risk-"

"Christ. You've taken me this far-" He broke off, shaking his head. "What are you trying to do? Kill me?"

"It's not my fault you weren't prepared."

Ridge made an explosive sound and made as if to get up off her but, quick as a flash, Lani's hands shot up and she grabbed his shoulders, refusing to let him leave. Like a revelation it came to her – if she let him leave now, like this, it would be all over.

"Wait," she whispered urgently. "Don't move. Just stay right here."

Ridge closed his eyes and dropped his head then he groaned. "Why?"

"I don't want you to go," she whispered. "Just stay. Please." As she spoke she reached around to slide her hands up and down his back, his answering shudder all the reward she needed.

His face pressed against the side of her neck, Ridge slumped over her. "Lani, don't do this to me," he said, his whisper sounding so broken and desperate that it made her heart ache. "I beg you, don't torture me like this."

Feeling guilty as hell, Lani slid both arms up to gather him to her. "It's okay, honey. It's okay," she whispered. "We're doing this."

He went stiff in her arms. "How?"

She stroked his back. "Ever heard of the withdrawal method? It's not the most reliable but whatever happens, we'll deal with it. Now come on. Make love to me."

His face still pressed against her, when he spoke his lips tickled her neck. "You're sure?"

She nodded. "Absolutely."

It was only after that reassurance that Ridge moved again. He shifted his body, settling it back over hers, positioning his hips so they rested between her legs.

Lani relaxed under him, opening to him, and when Ridge pressed his manhood against her moistness she wrapped her arms around him and pulled him close, letting him slide deep inside.

And then he began to move, slowly at first, as if testing her, seeing how much she could take. But then when she did not pull back he moved faster, sliding into her, moving with a smooth and steady rhythm that picked up speed as he stroked. Soon he was thrusting into her, his body seeming to move of its own accord, his eyes clenched shut, his breathing tight and labored, his grip tight on her shoulders.

And Lani was moving with him, her body rocking, her hips thrusting up to meet him. The heat in her body climbed till she was burning up with the passion that raged between them.

Lani was so caught up in the heat of the moment that when Ridge pulled away and out of her she gasped. "What?" Her eyes flew open as she reached for him but he'd rolled away, panting, eyes clenched tight, trembling like he had the ague.

"Please come back." She was reaching for him but he put up a hand, stopping her cold.

"Don't move." He spoke through clenched teeth. "Don't...move." He was sucking in deep breaths, looking like he was struggling to stay in control.

How could she have forgotten? Ridge had withdrawn just in time and she'd been there, like an idiot, calling him back, putting him under even more pressure.

With effort that seemed almost super-human Ridge drew in a long, shuddering breath and then he opened his eyes. "I need a shower," he said, his voice choking. "A real cold one."

And then, before she could move, he was up and out of the bed, leaving her cold and lonely as she lay there, watching him head once more for the bathroom.

And as she lay there, feeling ashamed at what she'd put him through, Lani knew in her heart that something had changed, something on her side, at any rate. She'd opened herself to taking a chance with Ridge, the biggest chance of all. Right at this moment there was the chance that she was carrying his baby and, as far as she was concerned, there would be no regrets.

And next time, when they were ready to make love again, things would be different.

The question was, after she'd made Ridge suffer so, would there be a next time?

CHAPTER EIGHT

One week and counting.

For the past week Ridge had made sure to stay out of Lani's way, even going so far as to deliberately get home late at night after she'd gone to bed. It was better that way. After the taste she'd given him of her delectable body, coming home to see her was nothing but torment. How did she expect him to go on living in the same house with her, see her each night, and not be able to touch her?

Okay, so he'd touched her, as intimately as you could get, but she'd put restrictions on him, denying him the ultimate pleasure, taking him ninety percent of the way and keeping him from that final release. He'd had a hell of a time holding it in. She couldn't have known how close he'd come to exploding inside her.

Thank the stars he hadn't, but he could make no promises for next time...if there ever was a next time. And the way she had him climbing the wall in frustration there'd better not be, because he knew he would never be able to hold back.

Ridge glanced at his computer screen. After seven o'clock. He was dead tired but he was too scared to get in the car and drive home. Yes, he wasn't going to tiptoe around it – he was running scared, and it was all the fault of that petite pixie with jet-black hair and ruby lips, the same one with the slim waist and full breasts that were so hard to resist. Even as he sat staring at the computer screen he could taste the strawberry tips-

Ridge jumped. The phone. His cell phone was buzzing in his trousers. He snapped his attention back to the present and dug into his pocket. When he glanced at the screen he saw that it was Lani.

He tapped the screen. "Yeah, Lani. What's up?"

"Ridge, are you going to be home soon? We need to talk." Her voice was breathless, like she was excited. Or was that worry he was hearing?

"Is everything okay?" he asked, straightening up.

"Everything's fine," she said. "In fact, everything's perfect. That's why I want you home so I can tell you about it."

Everything is perfect. That was the last thing he'd expected her to say, under the circumstances. "What's going on?" he asked.

"I'm not going to tell," she said, her voice turning cheeky, "until you get here. Now pack up your work and get your butt home."

Before he could answer she hung up the phone. Well, the lady had spoken. There was nothing to do but head on home and hear the great news she had to share.

As soon as he walked into the house Ridge called out her name. "Lani, I'm home. Where are you?"

"I'm down here," she called back and as he turned he saw her coming from the kitchen. She was all smiles which, for Lani, was not the norm.

"So what's the great news?" he asked, deciding to cut to the chase. He was never one for suspense.

"You won't believe it," she said, coming to stand right in front of him. "I found the source for a rare plant I've been hunting down for ages." She grinned up at him. "I'm leaving for South America in two days."

***

So this was Manaus, the capital of the Amazonas region. Lani flung her arms wide and twirled around and around in the hotel room. She was finally here in Brazil, home to a big portion of the Amazon jungle, the habitat that would provide her with the secret plant potions she craved.

It hadn't been easy, getting here. When she dropped the bombshell Ridge was surprised, which was to be expected. What she hadn't expected was for him to go ballistic and demand that she stay right there in Texas and send someone else.

"No wife of mine is going traipsing through some jungle," he'd declared. "Do you know how dangerous the jungle is?"

She'd laughed him off. "I'm hunting for plants," she'd told him, "not anacondas and alligators."

"That doesn't mean you won't find some along the way," he'd practically snarled. "You're not going."

"Oh, yes I am."

"No, you're not. Don't even think about it."

And so they'd had a huge fight that night until, probably realizing that she would never back down, he'd finally relented. Sort of. He'd finally accepted that she was going to Brazil but only, he said, if he went with her.

And so, to Lani's chagrin, she'd acquired a chaperon and not the most pleasant one either. He'd been a pain the entire flight, issuing warnings that she could do without. Now that they were at the hotel she had to thank the stars he'd gone downstairs to consult the concierge, giving her a well-needed break. Now she could relax.

She'd just gone out onto the balcony and plopped her bottom down on the tropical print sofa when she heard her cell phone ringing inside the living room. "Oh, Lord," she groaned as she got up, "let it not be Ridge calling to tell me not to drink the water or something like that." He'd kept her so busy with his safety tips that she hadn't even had time to take in the sights and scenery of the city.

She breathed a sigh of relief when she dug the phone out of her handbag and realized it wasn't him. "Hi Mom," she said as soon as she tapped the answer button. "How are you and Dad?"

"We're fine, as always," her mother said drily. "The question is, how are you? Since you got married you've spoken to your mother what, three times? Is this how it's going to be?"

"Oh, Mom, you know it's just because I've been busy. I think about you and Dad every day."

"That's not good enough. I want to hear from you, know how you're doing. Is that husband of yours treating you well?"

"Yes, Mother. Very well. There's nothing for you to worry about."

"Mmhmm." For some reason her mother sounded doubtful. "So if he's treating you so great why doesn't he let you call your mother?"

Lani rolled her eyes. Not that question again. "Mom, if I don't call often Ridge has nothing to do with it. It's not his fault that I'm busy."

"Oh. So it's your fault that you haven't been calling." Lani could hear the huff in Marie's voice.

"Yes, Mother. All my fault." Then, desperate to change the subject, she asked, "Did you and Dad see that play I told you about? Mama Mia. Did you go?"

"No, not yet, dear. But getting back to you, how are you feeling? Have you been woozy? Nauseous? Anything like that?"

"Nauseous? Why would I..." The words died in Lani's throat. "Mother, are you asking me if I'm pregnant?"

"Are you?"

"No, I'm not. What kind of question is that?" Lani couldn't believe her mother.

"Have you been working on it, though? Remember our discussion about grandbabies."

"Mother, I've only been married four weeks. And anyway, I explained the nature of my relationship." What part of 'business arrangement' didn't her mother understand?

"Well, be that as it may, you have to remember that you're almost thirty years old. Don't linger until your biological clock runs out, Leilani."

"No, Mom, I won't." Lani had to stifle a sigh. When her mother got like this it made no sense to argue with her. For an easy life it was better to just go along with what she said.

And then, to Lani's relief, her cell phone screen lit up with another call. "Sorry, Mom. I have to go. An important call's coming in."

Marie heaved a sigh. "Busy as usual. Okay, dear. Call me later."

It was the call Lani had been waiting for. "Yes? Aurelio?"

"Aurelio here, Dr. Donatelli. I was told you arrived in Manaus today."

"Yes, I'm here right now, at the Caesar. Thanks for connecting with me so soon."

"No problem, doctor. I know your time in Brazil is limited so I wanted to see if we can get started early. Tomorrow, if possible." The man's voice was coarse and deep but he sounded friendly enough. She'd heard he was an excellent guide and she was more than ready to take advantage of his services.

"Call me Lani," she said, "and tomorrow would be perfect. What should I bring?"

"I'll have the tents," he replied, "and if you give me your e-mail address I'll send you a list of items to bring. We have to be prepared for this trip."

"Of course." She gave him her e-mail address then wrote down the phone number he gave her.

"We will leave before sunrise," he said. "I will come to the hotel to pick you up."

"I'll be ready," she said and as they said their goodbyes she remembered she should have said they. Ridge would never let her go alone. But too late. Aurelio had already hung up.

When Ridge returned to the hotel room Lani was all smiles. "Guess what?" she said as he stepped in and closed the door behind him.

He gave her a look that was sharp with suspicion. "Whenever you have a happy grin on your face I know it's time to worry. What is it?"

"First thing tomorrow," she said, her smile widening, "we're heading into the Amazon jungle."

CHAPTER NINE

When he'd told Lani he would come on this Brazil trip with her Ridge had no idea what he would be getting himself into.

After she'd slapped him awake at the ungodly hour of four in the morning she'd loaded him up with a backpack that was bulky and heavy, even for him. It was like the woman had stocked him up with all the canned goods that could fit in the darned thing. And everyone knew how heavy canned goods could be.

Then they'd met her guide downstairs, a small, round-faced fellow who looked old enough to be Lani's grandfather. Where in the world she'd found him, Ridge had no idea. He just hoped the man didn't croak on them during the trip.

And then, as if that weren't bad enough, the vehicle he showed up with was cause for serious concern. It was an ancient looking Jeep, the sides eaten by rust and the tires so smooth they looked like you could go ice-skating with them. What kind of grip could tires like that have on the road? Ridge was of a mind to call a halt to the whole expedition but Lani was so bent on going that he didn't have the heart to burst her bubble.

The day still shrouded in darkness, they left the city and drove mile after mile until they were deep into the rural regions of Amazonas state. Because they stopped in Manacupuru for more supplies they didn't get to Igarape until late morning and by that time Ridge was starving. Lani and her guide, on the other hand, looked like they were surviving on fresh air. While he sat in the backseat, his stomach growling, they were in the front, busy chatting away. Finally, when it looked like they had no intention of pulling over for either a food or bathroom break, Ridge decided he had to speak up.

"Guys, what say we pull over the next chance we get? We must be low on gas by now."

Lani was the first to chirp up. "Oh, no. I'm good. And we've got lots of gas. Maybe half a tank."

It took Aurelio to come to the rescue. The elderly man glanced in the rearview mirror and must have seen the discomfort on Ridge's face because he nodded and gave him an understanding smile. "We will stop in fifteen minutes," he said, ignoring Lani and her bid to keep going. " An eating spot is just up ahead."

"Thank you." Ridge gave him a nod of gratitude. He seemed to have found some sympathy in Aurelio. Thank God for that.

An hour later, after a hearty meal of Feijado black bean stew and deep fried Pasteis filled with cod fish, the party set off again, this time with Ridge sitting up front beside Aurelio. It had taken the big meal for Lani to realize how tuckered out she was. When they got back to the Jeep she immediately claimed the backseat where she sprawled out. Within minutes she was fast asleep.

It was a good thing, too, because Ridge didn't know if her heart would have been able to take the rest of the journey. Although much of the terrain had been flat, this time Aurelio took them up a hill and along a winding dirt road so narrow that if they'd met another vehicle coming in the opposite direction he didn't know what they would have done. It didn't help that on one side of the road was the mountain wall and on the other was a steep precipice. As tough as he was – or used to think he was – his heart jumped into his throat and he gripped the seat so hard he thought his fingers would pop through the leather. He couldn't believe he'd lived thirty-four years on earth to come to this hellish place to meet his end.

It was an exhausted, drained and sweat-drenched Ridge who dragged himself out of the Jeep hours later. They'd come to a remote settlement, too tiny to even be called a village, and by this time it was pitch-black night. The few shacks that circled the clearing were in darkness and there was not a soul to be seen.

Lani, who'd woken up a couple of hours earlier, was the first to speak. "Where are we?" she whispered, like she thought her voice would be enough to wake the community.

"This is where we will camp tonight," Aurelio said, shutting off the engine. "Tomorrow we continue the journey on foot."

"Oh."

All of a sudden Lani didn't sound quite so excited. Just the opposite. There was a hint of fear in her voice, a rare show of vulnerability that made her seem almost childlike. Maybe it was the solid darkness that was doing her in. Whatever it was, it felt good to have her sidle close to him and reach for his hand.

When she slid her hand into his it reminded him of how tiny she was and he felt a surge of protectiveness flow through him. Even after that brutal journey he was glad he'd insisted on making the trip with her. She was a tough little cookie and an independent soul but that didn't mean she didn't need protecting. She was his wife and it was his duty to ensure her safety. It was a responsibility he took seriously.

When Aurelio went around to the back of the Jeep and began off-loading their gear Lani moved closer to whisper in Ridge's ear. "I wonder where everybody is? The place looks so deserted."

"This is probably just a camp ground for hikers," he speculated. "Maybe it's empty except when travelers pass through."

"You're probably right," she whispered back. "I'm going to guess we're the only ones here." There was a pause as she looked around, peering through the darkness. "Kind of scary-looking, too."

"As long as we're the only ones here," he said, giving her hand a squeeze, "we'll be all right."

Ridge soon had to leave Lani by the Jeep and go over to help Aurelio set up the tents. Within minutes of leaving her Lani was again by his side.

"Let me help," she said. "I'll hold the flashlight."

It may have been because she wanted to be helpful or it may have been because she didn't want to be too far away but Ridge didn't care. He was glad to have her close. It hadn't been easy, working on the tent and having to glance back at the Jeep every few seconds to make sure she was okay. Now, with her just an arm's length away, he could work much faster.

Within the hour they'd set up both tents and secured their gear. Aurelio bid them a cheerful goodnight then disappeared inside his tent, leaving Ridge and Lani to their own devices. With the most logical next move being bed and sleep they rolled out their sleeping bags inside the tent that had seemed fairly spacious until they had to fit two sleeping bags in it with all their stuff. It ended up being a tight squeeze but they made it work. At one point Ridge thought of suggesting that they share just one sleeping bag but then he ditched the idea. The last thing he wanted was to trigger a fight. He could imagine they would have a happy spectator in Aurelio.

In the end none of that mattered because they were so exhausted that they both crashed on top of the bags, boots and backpacks and bottles of water scattered all around them. Ridge didn't know himself until next morning after the sun had come up and Lani had already slipped out of the tent.

He sat up, his back aching from his firm bed of solid ground. Rubbing his eyes, he yawned then pushed forward onto his knees and crawled out of the tent. When he peered out it was to see Lani and Aurelio already in hiking gear, looking like they were ready to head out.

"Hey," he called out, "are you guys leaving? Without me?"

At the sound of his voice Lani turned and lifted her hand in a little wave. "You're awake. Finally. The way you were snoring away we thought we wouldn't see you till lunch time."

Ridge frowned. "What time is it?"

Aurelio glanced at his watch. "Sixteen minutes after seven."

"But that's still early. What about breakfast? Aren't we going to eat first?"

"We already ate," Lani said, shifting the backpack on her back and looking like she didn't want to linger a second longer. "You can stay and eat while Aurelio and I hit the trail."

"Not on your life." Ridge scrambled out of the tent and headed toward the stream. "You stay put. I'm coming with you."

After much grumbling on Lani's part while he washed then grabbed some cold cereal, they headed out. Now he was in a much better mood. His stomach was halfway full and the fresh, clean air felt good on his face.

"Remind me again why we didn't book into one of those jungle lodges? I hear they're all inclusive."

"Because," Lani said, giving him an impatient look, "this is not a tourist trip to the jungle. This is business. We're going to a remote region of the rainforest."

"This area sees few humans," Aurelio said. "It is only the serious ones who come this way. This trek, it is not easy."

Ridge gave Lani a wry grin. "Sure you can handle it?"

She grinned back. "Don't you worry about me," she said. "It's you who should worry about keeping up."

Lani's words turned out to be only too true. Aurelio led the way, chopping at bushes as he made a path for them through the thick foliage. Lani followed close behind and Ridge brought up the rear. It was tough, being a foot taller than the two people ahead of him. Aurelio might think he was clearing the way and his efforts worked for him and Lani but definitely not for Ridge. The path that the little man was clearing was not high enough for Ridge, not by a long shot. He'd been slapped in the face by enough swinging leaves and branches to gather the bruises to prove it.

Unfortunately, after all that hiking, that evening they returned to camp empty-handed. He could see the disappointment on Lani's face.

"Tomorrow we find some good samples," Aurelio reassured her. "We go deeper next time. Two days walk, not one."

The guide's declaration made her perk up considerably but Ridge frowned. "Two days? So we won't come back to camp tomorrow night?"

Aurelio shook his head. "No, we must go deep, deep into the forest. Two days' walk, maybe three."

"What the..." Ridge turned to Lani. "You never told me we would have to go through all this."

She shrugged, looking unconcerned. "I didn't know but if Aurelio says we have to go deeper then that's what we'll do."

"I told you, you should have let someone else make the trip," he grumbled. "What about that guy who works for you? Chris whatever-his-name-is. This is no place for a woman."

Lani gave him a mischievous grin. "Or maybe you should say, this is no place for a pampered rich guy who can't manage jungle living."

That shut him up. It would be a long time before Lani heard another complaint out of him. He would not give her the satisfaction of calling him soft.

And so the next morning he made it a point to be up and ready before Aurelio and Lani even began to stir. They wanted a mountain man? They would get one. By the time Aurelio crawled out of the tent Ridge had the coffee ready and when Lani finally peeped out he'd finished making a full breakfast of beef jerky and powdered eggs.

"Hmm, smells good," she told him and then she gave them a demonstration of her healthy appetite when she wolfed down two platefuls. Even Aurelio raised his eyebrows in surprise. She was such a tiny girl. Who could have guessed she could sock away that much grub?

But Lani must have known what she was doing when she ate that much because they were three hours into their journey when Ridge began to feel the hunger pangs. Of even greater concern was the fact that it looked like Aurelio and Lani had gotten their second wind and had no plans to stop any time soon. But Ridge was not about to beg them to stop. He'd already resolved that he wasn't going to come off like a wimp and if it meant sucking in his gut and suffering through his hunger then so be it.

It was another two hours before their guide called the hike to a halt. By this time Ridge was so hungry he wasn't even feeling the pangs in his stomach anymore. They'd moved up to his head and now he was suffering from a splitting headache. Damn him for being too stubborn and too stupid to speak up when it would have made a difference. Now that they'd come to a halt all he could do was slide the rucksack off his back and collapse onto the ground beside it.

"This is great," Lani said as she came to sit beside him. "Aurelio said we're getting there."

Ridge only grunted and reached for his canteen. He was in no mood to hear how good they were doing when he felt like crap.

"It's a good thing I did all those work-outs in preparation for the trip. I spent my lunch hours at the gym. I told you about it, didn't I?"

Ridge gave her a sour look. "No, you didn't. How come I didn't know you were supposed to do special preparation for this trip?"

"Oh. I guess," she glanced away, looking thoughtful, "I guess it was because it wasn't in the plan for you to be on this trip."

In response to that Ridge only grimaced.

Later, though, after their break he began to feel a whole lot better and actually kept up with the two 'Energizer Bunnies' ahead of him. And on top of his admiration for Lani's stamina he now had a healthy dose of respect for Aurelio. Despite his years the man had energy that would rival someone half his age. Maybe the old man was already consuming whatever plant Lani was seeking, the one she felt would be the answer to so many ills. Whatever Aurelio's secret was, Ridge knew he had to get some.

That night when they made camp as the twilight turned to dusk, Lani came to sit by him and as she leaned against him and he felt the warmth of her body against his Ridge was tempted to wrap his arms around her but he resisted the urge. He still didn't have a good handle on Lani and her moods. He decided not to make any move and just let her take the lead. That was the safest way.

She didn't take things any further, seeming comfortable just relaxing against him, probably not realizing the way she was ratcheting up the tension in his body. He was actually relieved when she moved away, deciding to make it an early night. He waited until she'd fallen asleep before stretching out on the leaves beside her.

Next morning they were up early, ready to take on the last lap of the journey. With their new burst of energy from being so close it didn't take them long, only a few hours, so that by the middle of the day they had reached their destination. Slowly, almost reverently, Aurelio approached the waterfall.

"It is a special kind of fern," he said, his voice hushed. "It grows in the caves behind this waterfall. We must approach it very carefully."

"We have to go through the water?" Lani looked doubtful.

Aurelio shook his head. "No, there is another way. I know a path that goes behind it, but it is dangerous." He glanced at Ridge. "You will hold her as we cross?"

"You bet." Ridge reached out to take hold of Lani but she shook off his hand.

"Not yet. We're not even there." Then she cocked an eyebrow. "And I might have to be the one holding on to you. I'm not a novice at mountain climbing, you know."

Ridge didn't even bother responding to that one. He was just glad she didn't seem scared at the prospect of climbing behind a pounding cascade of water.

After they'd refreshed themselves they started off toward the waterfall. The closer they got the louder the torrent sounded in their ears. The water was pounding as it fell to the rocks below, sending sprays of water high into the air, its deafening roar making it impossible for them to hear each other speak. They were left to communicate by hand signals.

Within minutes they were dripping wet from the spray but they kept going, Ridge staying close to Lani in case she stumbled.

Soon Aurelio was waving them on, directing them behind a wall of bushes so thick it was hard to see farther than a few feet ahead. Their guide did not slow his pace and Lani and Ridge had to hustle to keep up.

Then came the hard part. Aurelio signaled to them to be very careful on the rest of the path with its loose rocks along the winding trail. What made it worse, the trail led them onto a ledge which was little more than three feet wide with nothing but a drop of over a hundred feet on one side. It was along this treacherous path that they had to go to get to the entrance to the cave.

Signaling to Lani to press her back against the wall, Ridge went ahead of her, sidling sideways, holding her hand as she followed every step he took. He could feel her palm grow moist in his hand but he didn't relax his grip on her until they had shuffled the four or five yards it would take to get them to safety. With the water cascading in front of them and water droplets flying everywhere it was hard to see but Ridge gritted his teeth and kept going until he was finally able to pull Lani to safety within the cavern that lay behind the waterfall.

As soon as she was in she fell to the ground, laughing. "Whew. That was exhilarating. Did you look down?"

Ridge drew his arm across his forehead, wiping away the water droplets, then he gave her a look of disbelief. "You're kidding, right?"

"No. I looked down."

Ridge didn't know what to make of that. The girl had a lot more backbone than he'd thought. Heck, she was braver than he was. He hadn't looked down and he had no intention of trying it on the way back, either.

Aurelio was already far inside the cave and as soon as Ridge and Lani realized they'd been left behind they hurried to catch up.

"Come, Miss," he called out. "It is down here."

Lani picked up pace, breaking into a run until she'd caught up to her guide. "Is it much farther?" she asked, her voice breathless.

"No, we are almost there."

They rounded a corner, disappearing from Ridge's view, forcing him to pick up speed so he wouldn't lose sight of them. It wasn't easy going on the slippery surface of the cave floor and if he fell, a big man like him, it wasn't going to make a pretty picture. So he hurried along, but gingerly.

Just as he turned the corner he heard Lani cry out. "At last. Oh, my Lord. There's so much."

He was just in time to see her gazing up at a huge wall covered from top to bottom with thick ferns, their leaves giant in size. She reached out a hand to touch one of the leaves.

"Wait." Ridge hurried toward her. "There could be anything back there." He shone the flashlight on the spot she was about to touch, training the beam on the leaves. "Let me check it out first before you touch anything."

It took only a few minutes for Ridge to give Lani the all-clear and then she started plucking the leaves and dropping them into a big black bag she'd carried just for the purpose. Aurelio held the flashlight while she gathered her select specimens and soon the plastic bag was full. Then she forced the bag into her backpack.

Ridge watched her close it carefully then pass it to Aurelio to carry. He shook his head. "So you're telling me we came all the way to Brazil, risking life and limb on the edge of a precipice, for this? A bag of weeds?"

"Not weeds. Ferns." She threw him a caustic glare.

"And you couldn't have hired someone to come do this for you?"

"No. I had to do it myself. There aren't many people in Brazil who would take this kind of risk."

"Of coming all this way and climbing behind the waterfall?"

"No, of touching a plant that's bewitched."

"Be...what are you talking about?"

"Didn't you notice Aurelio hasn't touched the stuff even though he took us here? Most of the locals consider it bad luck to touch it. That's why I sealed it in the plastic bag before putting it in my backpack."

Ridge expelled his breath then planted his fists on his hips as he glared down at her. "So the almost two hundred million people in Brazil see it fit to avoid this plant but you decide you're too smart to follow their example?"

"Oh, come on, Ridge. It's just silly superstition, plain and simple. Do you think I'm going to let that stop me?" She shook her head. "The healing potential of this plant is too great for me to let local folklore get in the way."

"I see," he said, drawing out the word. "Dr. Fearless to the rescue."

She grinned. "If you want to call me that I'll take it. I've been called worse."

Ridge gave a snort of exasperation. Was this woman afraid of nothing? He turned, pointing the beam of light back the way they'd come. "Come on. You got what you came for. Now let's get out of here."

He marched forward, ready to get the hell out of there and back to civilization but he'd forgotten one critical thing. The slimy floor of the cave was as slippery as an oil slick. He took two steps and the next thing Ridge knew his left foot slipped and then his other leg shot out from under him and he was tumbling backwards, the flashlight flying out of his hand to slam into the cave wall. He only had time to let out a yell before he fell backwards to the cave floor.

"Ridge!"

Lani's scream was the last thing he heard before everything went black.

CHAPTER TEN

"Oh, my God. Ridge. Oh, no. Aurelio, help him. Where are you?" Lani cried out in the darkness, shock shooting through her even as the icy fingers of fear encircled her heart. "Ridge. Say something!"

She flung her arms wide, trying to get her bearings in a darkness so solid it felt like a heavy weight pressing into her.

There was a sudden flash of light and Aurelio appeared. "I found my flashlight, Doctor," he said. "His shout. He made me drop it. I am here now."

He ran forward to shine the light down on Ridge who lay flat on his back before them.

Lani scrambled forward and dropped to her knees. "Ridge. Oh, Lord. Ridge. Open your eyes. Please."

No response.

"Ridge. Please, honey." Lani pressed her fingers to his neck, desperate to find his pulse.

"He is not conscious, Miss. He cracked his head on the ground." Aurelio laid his flashlight on a rock so it would shine down on Ridge and then he reached out to loosen the collar of the prostrate man's shirt. "We must let him breathe," the elderly man said. "Give him air so he can come back to us."

Lani began to help Aurelio, loosening buttons like he was doing, and as she did she drew in a shuddering breath. It was all her fault. She should never have let Ridge come on this trip. Worse, she should never have let him hike deep into the jungle with her and Aurelio. If she'd made him stay back at the camp none of this would have happened.

Her heart quaking at the sight of him lying there hurt, Lani leaned down to press her ear to Ridge's chest. She drew a breath of relief when she heard his heart beating a slow, steady rhythm. And then she heard him groan and it was the sweetest sound she could have heard right then. Ridge was coming around.

"Ugh. What happened?" His words were followed by a moan and he lifted his hand to his head.

"You slipped," Lani told him. "You fell and hit your head." She reached out a hand and pressed it against his shoulder as he shifted. "No, don't get up. Not yet." Sitting back on her haunches she stripped off her jacket and rolled it up into a ball then, ever so gently, she lifted his head and slipped the makeshift pillow beneath. That done, she looked back at his face. "How are you feeling?" she asked anxiously. "Are you in pain?"

Ridge groaned again. "Outside of feeling like a boulder just slammed into the back of my head, no, I'm fine."

Lani's face broke into a smile, albeit a tentative one. "The fact that you still have a sense of humor tells me you'll survive." Relief began to loosen the vice of anxiety that had gripped her heart. She was so focused on Ridge that she didn't even remember their travel companion until he dropped to his knees beside her, a bottle of water in his hand.

Aurelio held the bottle to Ridge's lips. "Sip," he ordered. "It will settle your head."

Ridge groaned again but he didn't resist. He'd taken only a few sips when Aurelio pulled the bottle away.

"No, not too much," he said. "We wait a bit and then I give you some more."

With a sigh Ridge settled back against his balled-up-jacket pillow and closed his eyes.

Lani threw Aurelio a worried glance. "What if he falls asleep?" she asked. "Is that safe? If you have a concussion you're supposed to stay awake, right?"

"Con...what is that?" Aurelio gave her a puzzled look.

"Never mind," she said, reaching a hand out to touch Ridge. "I'll keep him awake."

"No, he is not sleeping," Aurelio said, shaking his head. "He is resting. Let him rest. Very important." Now Lani didn't know what to do – listen to Aurelio who had years of experience behind him and should know a thing or two, or go with her gut?

In the end the gut won out. Ignoring her guide, wise though he might be, Lani leaned down again, this time to whisper in her husband's ear. "Wake up, Ridge. Open your eyes. I want you to look at me."

The only answer she got was a deep sigh.

Wanting to waken him but in the gentlest possible way, Lani dipped her head to touch Ridge's lips with hers.

Immediately, she got the reaction she sought. Like her touch lit a spark within him Ridge gave a soft moan, his lips parting to receive her kiss, his arms sliding up to wrap around her, pulling her down on top of him.

Before she knew what was happening Ridge was the one in control, capturing her head with his hand, deepening the kiss. And it didn't seem to matter that they had an audience. Ridge was kissing her like a man drowning, drawing from her the air he so desperately needed.

When he finally released her, allowing her to draw back and away from him, he was panting slightly, like the kiss had been enough to drain him of his energy. But he was smiling. "Thank you," he whispered. "I needed that."

And just seeing him like that, still on his back but more importantly, with a smile on his face, made Lani smile right back. From the look of things he was going to be all right.

Wanting to give Ridge time to recover from his injury they didn't leave the cave until a couple of hours later and even then they moved at snail's pace. Not wanting to take any chances Lani insisted that Ridge get down on hands and knees and crawl along the ledge to safety. She couldn't risk him standing upright then getting woozy and toppling over the edge. Just to make sure he would comply she led the way, dropping to her hands and knees ahead of him and crawling out of the cave and along the length of the ledge with Ridge close behind. This time it was Aurelio who brought up the rear but he didn't join in with the knee crawl. He just waited until they'd crossed and then he walked across, as easy as pie.

Now came the hard part. Ridge had been the one carrying the bulk of the gear but with the crack he'd taken to the head there was no way he could manage that. Lani tried to get the bag onto her back but it was too bulky. In any case, Aurelio had given her such a sour look when she'd grabbed Ridge's bag that she could guess he never would have allowed her to hike back to camp with it.

They ended up having to go through all the bags, ditching as much as they could survive without, and then with the bags half as light as they'd been on the way up Aurelio took Ridge's rucksack, Lani took Aurelio's and Ridge took hers. She didn't have the heart to tell him how comical he looked with her little bag on his back.

It was slow going even though Ridge insisted he was fine. Neither Lani nor Aurelio wanted to push him too much so even when he trudged on ahead of them they hung back, forcing him to slow down. Eventually he got the message.

When the sun set that evening they were only a third of the way back to camp but that was the best they could do, under the circumstances. After refreshing themselves by the stream that was the tail end of the waterfall they'd left far behind they settled down for an early night.

Lani curled up beside Ridge and long after she could hear Aurelio's snores she just lay there, holding her exhausted husband in her arms.

He'd had a rough day. Although he'd played brave she'd seen the strain on his face and heard his labored breathing. It must have taken all his strength to keep going.

And so she lay there on the bed of leaves, his head nestled in the curve of her shoulder, and as he slept she stroked his hair, knowing that he wasn't even aware of her caress but happy she could do it, anyway.

And maybe it was a good thing he slept, giving her the freedom to explore him to her heart's content. Maybe if he'd been awake she would have hesitated. But now, with him lost to the world, she let her fingers curl in the dark silk of his hair then slip down to caress the curve of his jaw, now rough and sexy with unshaven hair. She let her hand slide down to stroke the strong column of his neck then steal inside his shirt where she splayed her fingers over his heart, feeling the reassuring thump and reveling in his warmth.

She began to draw her hand out, her fingers brushing his nipple on the way, and it was when she heard his gasp that Lani realized that Ridge was wide awake.

Her gaze flew to his face and she saw that he was looking down at her, his face all but hidden in the shadow of night, his eyes blazing with a fire so intense it made her shiver with awareness.

Lani didn't move her hand any farther. She didn't get the chance.

Ridge reached up and covered her hand with his, pressing it into his chest like he was branding it into his skin. Then he reached down to capture her arms and pull her up his body until her face was level with his. "I want you," he whispered, his voice urgent. "Now."

Lani sucked in her breath, her eyes widening in surprise. "But... Aurelio," she whispered back.

"Then we'll go," he answered, "far enough where we'll be alone." He made as if to rise but Lani pressed her body down on his, trying to hinder his movement.

"But is it safe?" she asked then looked around at the thick, dark, mysterious bushes that surrounded them. "This is the jungle, after all."

"We won't go far," he whispered. "Just far enough."

"I don't know," she began, but that was as far as she got because he was up on his feet before she'd even gotten the words out and he was pulling her up beside him.

"Come."

That was all he said and then they were tiptoeing away from the fire Aurelio had built, away from their temporary safe haven.

And although Lani wanted him badly she couldn't help wondering if they were being the worst idiots in the world. Even as she felt her heart quicken in anticipation, the thought did cross her mind - was sex with Ridge really worth the risk of being found by a jaguar? She guessed she would soon find out.

***

Ridge was no fool. He wanted Lani so bad he could taste her but he didn't want her so bad he would put her life at risk. As he was rising he'd slipped his hand under the backpack he'd tucked under his head, sliding the Bowie knife out, and then as he took her hand to turn her away he slid it into the back of his trousers. In the darkness she wouldn't have seen his move. No need to scare her unnecessarily.

Then, silent as a snake so as not to wake Aurelio, he led her away from the clearing and into the grassy alcove he'd found earlier that evening. Unnoticed, he'd slipped away from his travel companions soon after they'd taken their dip in the stream and upon finding the secluded spot he'd immediately thought it would be the perfect place to get away. The vines surrounding it formed a net of leaves so dense it would be hard for an animal to break through. At the same time, the section facing their camp area was sparse enough to give him a good view while hiding them from sight.

As soon as they stepped into the nook Ridge dropped to the grassy forest floor, pulling Lani down with him, his main intent to recapture her lips.

But she was having none of it. Instead of melting into his arms as he'd expected she would do, she resisted, letting him sink to the floor by himself. She shook her head. "You're not up to this yet," she said. "I can't let you."

Gazing up at her, he chuckled softly. "It's probably exactly what I need," he told her.

She shook her head again. "You stay right there," she said. "Let me do everything."

Ridge smiled, liking the sound of that. He was hot for her but if she would take the lead he didn't mind at all. And there would be one other plus to that. With her paying attention to him he could settle back and enjoy and still keep an eye on what was going on around them. You couldn't be too careful in the Amazon jungle.

Ridge lay back on his cushiony bed of green as Lani came to him. The subdued light from the faraway fire was like a halo to the back of her head, giving her a look so surreal that for just one moment it was like he was in the presence of an angel. He dared not take his eyes off her in case she disappeared like a figment of his imagination.

With the golden glimmer behind her Lani leaned down, her hair shiny-black and glistening in the light, and in answer to his silent plea she pressed her lips to his. He responded greedily, molding his mouth to hers, sucking hungrily on her lower lip. Too soon she was pulling away but he expelled a soft sigh of relief when she drew the satiny petals of her lips down his neck, sending sweet shivers running up his body.

But she didn't stop there. Like she wanted to taste every inch of his skin she quickly loosened the buttons of his shirt, tracing her lips over his chest as she went, going lower then across where she covered his left nipple with the soft velvet of her tongue.

Bold as brass she threw his shirt open as he lay back on the leaves but thankfully she didn't divest him of his buttons this time. Not pausing, she kept kissing his chest then his abs, moving lower until her breath was tickling the hairs just below his navel.

Ridge tensed, feeling himself grow even harder in his trousers, his stiffness calcifying into solid rock. He wanted to reach out and hold her but, not wanting to break the spell, he clenched his fists at his sides and waited for her to make the next move.

To his chagrin, her next move was one that made his body give an involuntary jerk. As Lani's lips slid lower still to graze the skin just above his waistband his hips jerked up, almost as if to meet her caress. He had to grit his teeth and slowly, deliberately, lower his butt back down to the ground.

She didn't even give him a chance to recover. Her hands moving quickly, her fingers deft and sure, Lani pulled the trouser button then had the zipper down in no time.

Shock ran through Ridge when she slid her hands inside and pushed down, leaving him with no option but to lift his hips again, this time to facilitate her goal of removing the bottom half of his clothing.

She pulled his trousers down, almost to his knees, leaving his loin area covered by nothing but the thin cotton of his underpants. Not that the darned thing was doing much good in concealing his state of arousal. His dick was so hard it formed a tent in his boxers, one that would send a weaker woman running.

But not Lani. To his surprise, she didn't stop there. In another second she curled her fingers over the waistband of said underpants and was pulling it down slowly, inch by inch, teasing him like she was intent on driving him crazy. And as if that weren't bad enough, with every inch the fabric moved down his hips, her tantalizing lips followed.

His hips jerked again. Jesus, he couldn't help it. His body was anticipating a caress he dared not imagine. His eyes clenched tight now, his head pressing back into the leaf bed, Ridge was breathing hard, dying a slow death as he waited.

And, God help him, if some animal showed up just then he probably wouldn't be able to move a muscle. He had to stay there. He had to know what she would do next.

And then, like she could guess the intensity of his torment, she made her move, pulling the shorts all the way down, exposing his hardness to her gaze.

He'd thought she would drop her eyes, maybe even pull back, but she was staring at him, her look surprisingly bold and unashamed.

She leaned forward again, making him suck in his breath, and it was at that moment that he heard it, a soft hiss that made his body go rigid.

Before Lani could move another inch Ridge's hand shot out to grab her upper arms and lift her off him then in one smooth move he was up, taking her with him, lifting her high off the ground. His free hand flew to his back and he grasped the handle of the knife still stuck in the back of his boxer shorts. "What are you doing?" Lani squeaked, clinging to his neck. "Put me down."

"Not yet." His arm locked around her waist, Ridge peered down at the leaves beneath their feet. "I thought I heard something. A snake, maybe."

Lani gasped. "A snake? Jesus."

"My thought exactly." Ridge grimaced. "Hold this." He passed the knife to her, freeing his hand so he could drag his trousers up over his butt and pull up the zipper. He had one more quick look down and then he was striding out of there, making a quick exit before he put Lani in any danger.

At the sound of his footsteps approaching Aurelio jerked up, looking surprisingly alert for a man who'd been wakened from a deep sleep. And, like Ridge, his first reaction was to reach for his knife.

"You guys okay?" he asked, quickly jumping to his feet.

"We're good," Ridge said, not wanting to scare the fellow, then just so he could help them be on guard he said, "I thought I heard a snake back there." By this time they were close to the fire, safe enough where he could lower Lani to the ground. "Didn't see anything, though."

Aurelio made as if to go check but Ridge stopped him. "No need," he told their guide. "We'll be right here by the fire. Chances are, it won't venture this close."

Aurelio looked relieved and sank back down onto his mat. Then, muttering something in another language he lay back down, curled up on his side and promptly went back to sleep. Or so it seemed. He'd closed his eyes and was breathing softly and deeply like he was in the comfiest of beds.

Taking Lani's hand, Ridge led her over to the other side of the fire and helped her down onto her mat. She tried pulling him down with her but he resisted.

Ridge shook his head. "I think we've had enough excitement for one night." He could see the disappointment on her face but as much as he would love to finish what they'd started he would not change his mind. They would just have to wait until they got back to an environment that would hold no surprises of the tropical-jungle-animal kind.

And so, slightly annoyed with himself for being so sensible, Ridge trudged back to the bed of leaves on the ground – alone.

CHAPTER ELEVEN

Next day the travel party made much better time on the trek back to their campsite. While Ridge was not one hundred percent back to normal – a slight headache persisted – he was good enough for them to pick up pace and by nightfall they'd covered twice the distance they'd done the day before.

Aurelio gave them a satisfied smile. "Tomorrow we will see our tents by noon."

Ridge cocked an eyebrow. "Wishful thinking, don't you think?" he muttered to Lani. "Didn't he also say we have another twenty miles to go?"

Lani nodded. "Yeah, and if we hit the road early and pick up our pace just a little bit we can be there by lunchtime."

Ridge looked at her askance. "Just how early?"

She shrugged. "We could head out about four."

"While it's still dark? I don't think so."

So the next morning they didn't head out quite as early as Lani had suggested which meant they didn't get to their camp quite as early as Aurelio had planned. Still, three o'clock in the afternoon was pretty good as far as Ridge was concerned. He drew in a deep breath of air and spread his arms wide. "Back to semi-civilization," he said. "I never thought I'd be so glad to see our tent."

Lani smiled. "Me, too. It's like our home away from home."

Aurelio spent the afternoon catching wild game then roasting the birds over a campfire. That evening they had a cooked meal for the first time in days and it left them all licking their fingers.

"Tomorrow we head back down to the village," Aurelio said. "But today we rest." And, as if taking his own advice, he wandered off to disappear inside his tent.

That left Lani and Ridge to their own devices and it was only six o'clock. "So what do we do now?" Lani asked.

Stupid question. Of course Ridge had a ready answer for that one. "I can think of one thing that's sure to keep us entertained," he said with a wicked grin.

She only chuckled and shook her head. She wasn't going to go there with him, not at this early hour. And definitely not while Aurelio might only be half asleep. "Want to take a dip in the river?" she asked. "I'll race you."

"Nope," he said from where he lounged on the ground beside the campfire-cum-barbecue pit.

"Oh, stop being so lazy," she chided. "Let's go take a swim."

"Seeing that I don't wish to be eaten by alligators I'll just skip the river run and stick to the little stream we used last time."

Lani gave a snort. "Coward."

"Mmhmm," he conceded. "A coward who plans to live to see another day."

Well, since you put it that way..." She got up and ducked into the tent then came out with a towel and a change of clothing. "Come on, then. What are you waiting for?"

Minutes later they were by the stream and although Lani had played brave, at the last minute she chickened out and told Ridge they would have to bathe separately.

Shaking his head, Ridge went off to sit behind the rock, as instructed. "You are so weird," he mumbled, looking none too pleased that he'd been banished until she finished her bath.

Little did he know that it had nothing to do with her being shy about him seeing her naked. Quite the contrary. It had everything to do with her seeing him in the nude. She was so turned on by his body that she was liable to jump him right there in open air. And she couldn't afford to do that, not with the possibility of Aurelio walking over and seeing them in an intimate, not to mention very embarrassing, position.

Lani bathed and changed clothes in quick time then she called Ridge who came from behind his rock and began stripping before she even got the chance to take up her position in the spot he'd just vacated. "Hey, gimme a chance, will you? I'm not at the rock yet."

In answer, he shrugged out of the sleeveless undershirt that clung to his body, outlining every ripple and cut of his abs. "I'm not shy," he said. "I don't mind if you take a look." And then he laughed like he knew exactly what he was doing when he hooked his thumbs in the bottom of the undershirt and whipped it over his head in one smooth move, exposing his glistening, perfect abs to her view.

That was Lani's sign to get the heck away and off to her rock. They'd already had a scare out in the wild and if she didn't take herself away she'd be all over him and they would probably find themselves right back in that unsafe, lust-laden situation.

Ridge had been at his ablutions only a few minutes when there was a sudden crack of lightning. Lani jumped, so startled she leapt from behind her safe spot. And then she remembered something that made her race back to the stream, shouting Ridge's name.

"Get out of there," she yelled. "That was lightning. You shouldn't be in water when there's lightning."

Obviously Ridge didn't need to be told twice. In a flash he was out, giving her a full-frontal view of his nakedness, the sight she'd been trying so hard to avoid.

But now, in the urgency of the moment, it didn't matter. She just wanted him out of the water and safe.

"Let's get back to camp," he said, dragging on his clothes, but before he was done there was another lightning flash then the sound of a tremendous crack and the sky broke right open and gigantic drops of rain began tumbling down.

"Come on," Ridge yelled. "Let's get back to the tent." He grabbed her hand and ran, practically dragging her along with him. With his long legs it was hard to keep up so she wasn't surprised when he got frustrated and swung her up and into his arms then picked up speed as he barreled toward the safety of the tent.

They got back pretty fast but it still didn't make any difference. By the time they scrambled into the tent they were both soaking wet, their clothes clinging to their skin, hair pasted down on their faces.

And they were laughing.

"Goodness, that was scary," Lani said, shaking the raindrops from her arms. "I thought you might get electrocuted."

Ridge wiped the back of his hand across his forehead, pushing the wet strands off his face. "Thanks for the warning. It happened so fast I didn't even know what was going on." Then he caught his shirt between thumb and index finger and pulled the dripping fabric away from his skin. "This is no good," he said, and without ceremony he began to peel it off his body. In quick time his damp trousers were gone, too, leaving him in nothing but his shorts and even that didn't look too dry.

He looked over at her. "Is that how you're planning on going to bed? Soaking wet?"

Lani shook her head. She'd been so busy watching him that she hadn't even been paying attention to her own sorry state. Still kneeling by the sleeping bag she grabbed the edge of her blouse and pulled it up and over her head. And since she hadn't bothered to put on a bra that left her breasts open to his unwavering stare. That did not deter her. Like Ridge, she shucked off her pants so she was soon kneeling on the ground in nothing but her panties.

And then as the rain pounded on their tent Lani and Ridge stared at each other, the one kneeling on the left side of the sleeping bag and the other on the right.

Ridge was the one who broke the spell. "What say we finish what we started in the mountains?"

Lani smiled. She had no objection to that. She never took her eyes off him as she climbed on top of the sleeping bag and even when she pushed her panties off her hips her gaze still held his. With the coming of the rain and the clouds blocking out what was left of day, inside the tent was pretty dark but that did not stop her from seeing the desire plain as day on his face. Ridge wanted her bad and that knowledge was enough to turn all her burners on.

But he still hung back, which Lani could not understand, but just in case he'd suddenly turned shy she rolled across the sleeping bag and reached up to drag him down on top of it and on top of her.

"Wait," he muttered. "Are we going to do that withdrawal thing again? Because I don't think-"

"Shhh." She put her lips to his ear and began to nibble the lobe. "Don't worry about it."

"Listen," he said in a low grumble, "I don't want you to stop me in the middle of it. You're my wife. I want to enjoy you to the fullest."

"And I want you to shut up," she said and gave him a sharp nip to the earlobe as punishment. "Just shut up and enjoy."

He was still on top of her but at her words he relaxed against her, giving her free reign to explore the inner curves of his ear then slide her tongue to taste the rain-flavored skin of his neck.

When Ridge sighed she shifted beneath him and he took her cue, taking his weight off her and rolling over onto his back so she could explore him fully.

Lani didn't hesitate to take him up on his invitation. Climbing on top, she straddled his hips then leaned down to capture his lips in a kiss that stole all his air. Then when he was sufficiently weakened she moved down, letting her nipple graze his chest, taking pride in the way she was making the goose bumps rise up on his skin. Tonight, though, she wasn't going to linger. As the thunder rumbled outside their nylon tent and as the rain pelted its surface she went straight for her goal. She slid down Ridge's body and grabbed fistfuls of his boxers and dragged them off him, all the way down his legs and off his feet.

His final garment gone Lani was just about ready to climb back up his body but then she changed her mind. Why not take the scenic route?

And so she paused to plant a soft kiss on top of his foot, smiling when he did a little squirm in response. Next she moved up his legs, the soft hairs tickling her lips as she covered his shins, his knees and then his thighs with butterfly kisses, his soft sighs giving her ample reward.

She moved up along his side over the smoothness of his hips and up to his waist and then she reached up to capture his nipples between her fingers, pinching and taunting them until she had him writhing from the pleasure of it all.

Before he could recover she was back on top of him, straddling his hips but never releasing his stiff buds and as she felt the heat of his hardness pressing up against her moistened core she sank down onto it, impaling herself.

"Aah." Like he'd just been dropped into a vat of hot oil Ridge gasped out loud and his body jerked up, his back arching, his hips rising to drive him deeper inside. "Oh, Christ, you feel so good."

At her husband's strangled cry Lani's mouth went dry and she began to move, rocking her body on his, watching his chest heave as he sucked in air.

And as she moved Ridge began to move with her, meeting her stroke for stroke, his nostrils flaring as he sucked in air, his eyes never leaving her face.

Her hands splayed on the broad muscles of his chest, Lani rode him, taking all the pleasure she'd denied herself for so long.

Then, just as she approached her peak Ridge began to pant then he groaned out loud. "Lani, are you sure? I can't stop-" His voice broke off because instead of slowing down she quickened her pace, driving him on to that point where there would be no turning back.

Taking full control, Lani pushed until she was over the edge, tumbling down into a whirlpool of ecstasy, dragging Ridge along with her.

As he found his release Ridge uttered a groan so deep and then he was reaching for her, pulling her down and clutching her to him, crushing her against his chest.

For a long while they stayed like that, clinging to each other, their bodies shuddering in the final throes of ecstasy. And then, as the seconds passed into a minute and then two, their breathing calmed and they relaxed into each other's arms.

As Lani lay on top of Ridge, her cheek resting against his chest, he reached his hand up and gently stroked her hair. "Thank you," he whispered. "That was out of this world."

And as she listened to the words as they rumbled in his chest she didn't lift her cheek from where it lay just over his heart. Instead, she snuggled even closer, tightened her arms around Ridge, and smiled.

CHAPTER TWELVE

When Ridge awoke next morning, the memory of his pleasurable night with Lani still fresh in his mind, he smiled and reached out for her. He came up empty-handed. All he felt on the sleeping bag beside him was air.

Frowning, he opened his eyes. And then he smelled it – the familiar fragrance of fried eggs wafting into the tent. He smiled and relaxed back onto the padded surface of the sleeping bag. Lani had gotten off to an early start. She was busy making breakfast, playing little wife. He liked that. It actually made the tent and this wild environment feel like home.

Ridge rubbed the sleep from his eyes then got onto his hands and knees and crawled out of the tent. The earth was still damp from the rain but the sun was out and burning bright. The heat would be drying up the moisture in no time.

"Hey, honey. We've got breakfast ready for you."

Ridge looked up to see Lani looking fresh as a daisy in khaki trousers and white T-shirt, waving to him and smiling. Like she'd timed him perfectly she was holding a tin plate piled high with powdered eggs, strips of beef jerky and slices of bread she'd probably toasted over the open fire.

Ridge couldn't have asked for a better breakfast. Smiling, he got to his feet and lifted his arms in a leisurely stretch. "I'm so hungry I could eat all of that plus the plate it's on."

Lani laughed. "The food, you can eat, but not the plate. We're going to need it for later. Now go clean up then come get your breakfast before Aurelio and I gobble it down."

Ridge took her warning seriously. With a grin he headed off toward the stream but within minutes he was back and reaching for his plate. Then he found a comfortable seat on top of a rock and settled down to enjoy the meal his wife had prepared.

He'd gobbled down almost half the plate of food when he realized that Aurelio and Lani were just sitting there watching him, the same weird expression on each of their faces.

"What's the matter?" he asked, his voice muffled with the piece of toast he'd just bitten into. He swallowed. "Were you guys supposed to get some of this?"

"No, we ate. Waiting on you." Aurelio gave him a grave look.

"Oh." Ridge said the word, which made it seem like all was clear to him but he was more confused than anything. "Waiting on me to finish eating?"

"Yes," Aurelio said, "so we can go."

Ridge nodded. "Okay, cool. I'll hurry up. I guess you guys want to get back to civilization just as badly as I do." He tucked in, not wanting to hold up their departure from the campsite.

"Uh, Ridge," Lani said, her voice sounding strangely hesitant, "about that..."

As her words trailed off Ridge frowned then he lowered the forkful of eggs he'd just been about to put to his mouth. He had the sinking feeling he wasn't going to like what she was about to say.

She bit her lip then flashed him a guilty look. "We're not leaving camp today."

"What?" Ridge frowned and lowered his plate. "Why not?"

Lani clasped her hands behind her back, which made her look like a child caught in the middle of a naughty act. "Well, we decided to stay here a while longer and do some more exploring."

"We decided?" By this time Ridge's frown had descended into a full-fledged scowl. "You and Aurelio?" He didn't say the rest of what he was thinking but from the look on Lani's face he could see she knew exactly where he was going. She could read that he was pissed that their decision hadn't included him. "Not we," she said quickly. "I. I was the one who decided we should stay longer."

Ridge's eyes narrowed as he watched her. "May I ask why?"

Maybe Lani thought his question meant he was willing to have a discussion because her stance relaxed and she loosened the clasp of her hands and reached out to pluck a leaf from the bush beside her. "Aurelio was telling me about another plant," she said, "one I'd never heard of before. He said I can get some not far from here. If we just hike for eight miles east of here we'll get to the grove-"

"Are you out of your mind? After we risked our lives to get your plant samples you want to find more? You're a sucker for punishment or what?"

Eyes wide and her look earnest, Lani shook her head. "You don't understand, Ridge. Aurelio told me it's a healing plant, known in Brazil for ages. What if it's the answer to some of the diseases running rampant in our country?"

Ridge gave her a skeptical look. "I thought those other ones you got were the answer."

"We don't know. Don't you see? It could be anything. It could be the one Aurelio's telling me about."

As she called his name Aurelio stooped down, sat back on his haunches and began poking at the almost dead fire with a stick. He looked like he wanted to be anywhere but there right at that moment.

"Sounds like a wild goose chase to me," Ridge said with a snort. "If you ask me, the best thing we could do is pack up camp and head on out of here before more bad luck befalls us."

"Well, I didn't ask you," Lani shot back at him. "And what kind of bad luck are you talking about?"

"Didn't you say those bushes you got were bad luck? I got cracked on the head, didn't I?"

Lani gave him a look of pure exasperation. "That had nothing to do with it. You didn't look where you were going and you slipped. Now if you'd only paid attention-"

"So you're calling me careless now?" The rest of his breakfast forgotten, Ridge put the plate on the ground and stood up. "It was dark in there, and slippery. It could have happened to anybody."

"And that's exactly my point. It could have happened to any of us. It had absolutely nothing to do with bad luck brought on by my plants." By this time Lani was getting so worked up her chest was heaving.

But if she thought her show of emotion would sway him she'd better think again. "We're leaving," he said, "and not to go traipsing through the forest again. We're going back to the city. Today."

Lani's brows fell. "You can't tell me what to do."

Ridge gave her a cool stare. "You can't go if I don't let you." Then he gave her a mirthless smile. "You're not going into the woods unless I go with you. And I'm not going with you."

"I'm going," she snarled, "and you can just sit here and grow moss till I get back. I don't care." With that she stalked off, heading in the direction of the stream.

"I'm packing up," Ridge yelled after her. "When you get back we'll be ready to go."

She didn't bother to answer but just kept walking.

Ridge shook his head. Hothead, that was what she was. Why did she think she should always have things her way? He glanced over at Aurelio who still stooped by the fire, looking uncertain. "She doesn't understand that I'm doing this for her own good," he said, trying to downplay the quarrel and reassure their guide. "This place is dangerous. She got what she came for so it's best to just get on out of here before anything else goes wrong."

Aurelio nodded. "We go now," he said solemnly. "Don't push our luck."

"Now you're talking." Ridge gave him a nod of approval. If only his woman would get the point as easily as Aurelio did. Muttering to himself he strode toward his tent, ready to dismantle the thing and pack it into the Jeep.

And that was when the second stroke of bad luck befell him. Just as he went around the boulder to which they'd secured the tent Ridge stepped down onto a pile of pebbles. Loosened by the pounding rain of the night before, they shifted under his feet, making his ankle twist under him, sending him tumbling to the ground.

It was his yell that brought Aurelio hurrying to his side. "What is the matter? You are hurt?"

His face contorted in pain, Ridge looked up from where he'd fallen to the muddy ground. "God, this hurts. It feels like I sprained my ankle."

"Not good." Aurelio clucked his tongue, looking worried. "Not good." Then, like he was forgetting he was a hundred pounds lighter than Ridge and twice his age, he tucked his shoulder under the injured man's armpit and reached his arm behind his back to hoist him up.

"No, that's okay." Ridge pushed him off, but gently, and then he rolled over and onto his knees. "I'll crawl if I have to."

"No, you stay there." Aurelio got up. "I will go and find the doctor."

Ridge groaned and he was just about to tell Aurelio not to bother but the man had already disappeared into the brush. He could just imagine what Lani would say when she came back and found him like this. Clumsy, that's what she would call him, and careless. And if he answered her like he wanted to, then that would be the start to yet another argument.

By the time Aurelio came back with Lani, Ridge was back inside the tent, lying on top of the sleeping bag. His ankle hurt so much he had to grit his teeth to keep from groaning out loud.

He was in the middle of a suppressed moan when the flap of the tent was flung open and she tumbled in. "What happened?" she asked, looking more concerned than he'd expected. "Are you hurt bad?"

Ridge drew in a slow breath. "Aurelio told you what happened?"

"He said you slipped and fell."

He grimaced. That sounded more embarrassing than how it had actually happened. "I stepped on some loose rocks and they shifted. Made me twist my ankle."

"Oh." She didn't sound too impressed by his version of the story.

"Anyway," he said, eager to cover his embarrassment, "you know what that means."

"No. What?"

"It means I couldn't go on that eight mile trek with you even if I wanted to. And if I'm not going, you're not going."

That got him a glare from Lani. "You didn't want to go on the hike, anyway." Then she knelt down on top of the sleeping bag beside him. "You're right about not being in any condition to go but I'm sorry. That's not going to stop me."

"What are you saying? You're planning on leaving me in this condition and going into the jungle all by yourself?"

"I won't be by myself," she reminded him. "Aurelio will be with me."

"I already told you," Ridge said through gritted teeth, "you're not going anywhere." He didn't know which was more annoying now, the throbbing ache in his ankle or Lani and her stupid insistence.

"You can't stop me," she said, her look defiant.

"Oh, can't I?" Before she could move his hands shot out and he grasped her by the upper arms, dragging her down on top of him. "I'll keep you here all day and all night if I have to."

"Hey, let go." She was squirming on top of him now, doing more harm than good. She might not even know it but with her little body wriggling on top of him she was wakening the beast inside his pants. He was getting hard, real fast.

"Stop squirming, will you?"

"I won't," she said, panting as she tried to pull her arms free. "Not until you let me go."

"You're going to have a long wait."

Those words seemed to incense Lani because she began to squirm anew, for at least a full minute, and then she slumped down, exhausted.

As she lay on top of him Ridge chuckled deep in his throat. Sometimes it paid to be a man with enough muscles to keep a woman in her place.

He'd just begun to get comfortable with her nestled against his chest when Lani made a move he could not have anticipated. Sneaky as a snake, she slipped her hand up under his armpit and began to tickle until he was chuckling then laughing out loud, his grip on her loosening just enough that she was finally able to wrest her arms from his grasp.

Immediately, she popped up and jumped away from him and although he tried to grab her again it was too late. "I'm sorry," she said again as she backed away from him and out of the tent. "I'm going. I'll leave you with water and all the supplies you'll need. I'll be back in a few hours."

"Lani, don't play games with me. I said you're not going." Ridge's words fell on deaf ears or rather, absent ones, because by the time he got the words out Lani was gone.

Ten minutes later she was back with bottles of water, boxes of crackers, a couple of oranges and apples and some plums. "You can snack on these until we get back," she said. "I'll ask Aurelio to snare some game on the way back so we can fix you some dinner tonight."

"So you're going," he said, still not believing it. "You're leaving me here in my injured state?"

"Oh, you're a big boy," she said, giving him a wave of dismissal. "You'll be all right. And besides, we'll be back long before nightfall. I promise."

Ridge gave her a sour look. "And what am I supposed to do all day?"

"I've got a romance novel in my backpack. It's pretty good. One of those billionaire romance thingies."

Ridge gave her a scathing look. "I'm supposed to entertain myself with a friggin' romance novel for the entire day?"

"I told you, this one's pretty good. Now I really have to get going so I can be back in good time. I'll see you later."

He didn't get another word out. In a flash she was gone, leaving Ridge on his back with her sorry pile of food to one side of him and her romance novel bearing backpack to the other. Well, so much for being the man who called the shots.

After she'd gone he lay there for a good hour but then he got sick of it. There was just so much of lying still, listening to the birds in the trees, that a man could take. With a groan he rolled over onto his side, careful not to bump his injured ankle, and then he got to his knees. He crept over to the tent opening and peered out. Nobody. Nothing but the breakfast fire that was now just a pile of dead ashes and in the background, trees and bushes all around their clearing. It was so still out there he actually felt lonely. He just hoped the fact that the place was so quiet, no stray jaguar would come wandering in.

At the thought Ridge crept backwards, back into the tent, and made sure to pull his Bowie knife from under his pillow and slide it into the waistband of his trousers. If a jaguar was going to attack he wanted to at least have a fighting chance.

But then that thought led to another. Lani was out there in the jungle with only an old man to protect her. Godammit. Why did that woman have to be so stubborn? If he could have walked he would have been there by her side. She knew that. Why couldn't she have let well enough alone and just stayed at camp with him?

Two more hours passed and all Ridge could do was keep glancing at his watch. Had they reached their destination by now? Were they on their way back? His chest tightening with each thought of Lani out there in the woods, Ridge crawled to the tent flap and peered out again, knowing full well that they wouldn't be back yet, but just hoping for a miracle.

When the hunger pangs grew too strong Ridge munched on some of the crackers Lani had left then washed the tasteless meal down with bottled water. He crunched on one of the apples but when that was gone he turned away from the food. That was all he could stomach for the moment. How could he eat when he had no idea where Lani was just then and if she was safe?

Two more hours later, still no Lani and Aurelio. He'd tried distracting himself with the romance novel she had left him but even though it started out as good as she'd said it was, he kept stopping after every page, listening for her voice. Then in the middle of the story his mind would wander and then he'd have to start the page all over again. Finally, frustrated, he dashed the paperback into the corner and slumped back on the sleeping bag.

Several more hours later, after he'd ventured out of the tent a couple of times with a makeshift cruch, the sun was beginning to set and there was still no sign of Lani and Aurelio. And if Ridge had been worried before, now he was damn near frantic. Where the hell were they?

Raking his fingers through his hair he looked toward the east where they'd gone. It was almost night, not the time to be wandering around in the woods. What should he do now? It wasn't like he could call them on a cell phone, not all the way out here in this remote wilderness. The only way he could reach them was to follow them into the forest. But that didn't make a lick of sense. They'd gone east but where exactly? And now that it was getting dark, how the heck was he going to find them?

Muttering to himself again, Ridge shook his head. He had three options as far as he could see – head into the forest after them, take the Jeep and try to find his way back to the city, or stay put and wait for them to get back.

He didn't like any of them.

Half an hour later, when the moon began to shine its weak beam through the leaves, Ridge decided he could wait no longer. He'd stayed at camp long enough. Maybe too long. And even if he could get back to the city to round up a search party there was no time. Poor Lani could be in trouble even right at that moment. It was that thought that made Ridge decide to attempt the next-to-impossible. He was going into the forest to find them.

Making sure he still had his knife, Ridge grabbed his crutch and his flashlight and turned the beam toward the bushes on the east side. He began to hop out of the clearing, trying his best to put as little weight as possible on the ankle, but he stumbled and almost fell and the only way he could save himself was to stomp down hard on the sick leg.

Sweat popping out on his forehead as the pain shot up his leg Ridge sucked in his breath, clutched his stick closer and tried again. It took him a good three minutes just to get across the clearing and into the bushes that led to the stream. How in heaven's name was he going to do eight miles?

He shook his head. He couldn't think about that. He had to stay focused on his goal. He had to find Lani.

He'd just sucked in his breath, preparing himself to make another step, when he saw it. A light in the distance. The beam of a flashlight. And it was coming his way.

"Lani. Is that you? Aurelio? Answer me." Hobbling toward the light he peered ahead, flashing the beam of his own light. "Guys, talk to me."

And then he heard the sweet voice that made his heart swell with relief.

"Ridge. We're here. We're coming."

He heard the sound of branches breaking and leaves being slapped out of the way and then the footsteps as his missing travel companions came toward him.

Lani broke through the leaves to the left of him and when he saw her his heart jerked in his chest. He wanted to run to her but he couldn't so he just held his arms open wide and let her walk right into them. As soon as their bodies touched he wrapped his arms around his little woman and held her like he would never let her go.

"A little air, please."

It was only when Lani began to struggle that Ridge relaxed his hold and set her just far enough away so he could look down at her. "What happened? Where the hell were you guys?"

Aurelio, who by this time had come to stand close by, cleared his throat but just as he opened his mouth to speak Lani broke in.

"We're sorry, Ridge. We got sidetracked. I mean, I got sidetracked. We went to check on something else and the time... I didn't realize...it just flew by."

"You got...sidetracked." Ridge frowned. "You promised me you would be back in a few hours and then you got sidetracked?" He dropped his hands away from her, not believing what he was hearing. "Do you know what you put me through?"

"I know and I'm sorry but I thought you'd be all right, seeing that you were here in camp and you had everything you needed close by." She stepped back and away from him then shrugged and turned toward the camp. "And you're okay, aren't you? You seem pretty good to me."

It was that casual shrug that did him in, sending his blood boiling. "That's not the point. You told me you'd be back long before nightfall. And now you come strolling in at this time of night and that's all you have to say to me? You got sidetracked?"

By this time she was halfway to the tent but she stopped and turned. "It's no big deal, okay? We're here now and we're good and you're good and that's all that matters."

"No, it's not, dammit. You owe me a better explanation than that. You spend the entire day out in the bush then you stroll in as casual as you please, and give me some cock-and-bull story about getting sidetracked. Sidetracked? When you had me here wondering where the hell you were?" Ridge's voice was getting louder with each word he spoke but he really didn't give a damn. Lani had taken advantage of his semi-helpless state, staying out as long as she wanted, and she hadn't even spared him a second thought. And all that time he'd been worried sick about her. "And don't you walk away when I'm talking to you."

She'd started walking and now she waved her hand in the air like she was exasperated. "I don't need to listen to this. I don't see why you're making a mountain out of a molehill." She didn't stop walking until she reached the tent where she dropped her bag on the ground then crouched down and ducked inside.

And all that time Aurelio stood staring at them, from one to the other then back again, not saying a word.

It was darned embarrassing having the man you'd hired stand there witnessing your wife defying you. Maybe that was the reason Ridge's rage hit the roof. Crippled though he might be he was not about to have his woman disrespect him like that, and in front of an audience.

He set off toward the tent and though his ankle was no better than it had been when he'd set out before, now he covered the distance in half the time. "You get back here, Leilani Kent," he growled. "You don't walk away from me like that."

"Leave me alone." Her words were muffled by the tent but there was no mistaking the challenge in her voice.

"You don't want me to come in there," he said, deliberately making his tone threatening.

"Or else what?" came the angry retort.

That did it. Ridge let go of his crutch, dropped to his knees and pushed his way into the tent.

Lani was kneeling by the sleeping bag, stripping her shirt off, leaving her upper body in nothing but her sleeveless undershirt. "You seem to have forgotten something. I'm a grown woman and I don't have to answer to you."

"You're a grown woman who's my wife. That makes all the difference in the world."

"Is that so?" Her glare was fiery enough to scorch the skin.

"Yeah, that's so."

"Well, let me tell you something. From here on things are going to be different." She moved past him and lifted the tent flap like she was leaving but then she paused. "I'll fulfill my obligation and stay married to you till my prison term ends," she said, her voice cold, "but when we get back to Texas I'm moving out."

***

Lani and Ridge were back in Manaus. She had the plants she'd come all the way to Brazil for as well as the bonus samples Aurelio had gotten for her, and now she would be able to do all the experiments she'd planned, and more.

And Lani felt more miserable than when she'd been up to her ears in debt and in danger of being thrown out onto the streets. How could she have been such a bitch to Ridge? Now she was probably first on his list of 'Ridge's Most Hated'.

He'd left the hotel suite, saying he needed to go for a walk, but she knew it was because he didn't want to be around her. That was understandable, after the way she'd behaved in the jungle.

But he'd embarrassed her. He'd barked orders at her in front of Aurelio and that was why she'd lashed out. After the way she'd acted tough in the jungle she couldn't let their guide think she was a wimpy wife.

Lani heaved a sigh and walked out onto the balcony overlooking the garden. She'd done a stupid thing. She knew that now. She had to apologize and she had to come clean and tell Ridge the truth about what really happened in the forest.

But how, when he wasn't talking to her?

Her ringing cell phone cut into that thought and made her dash inside. Maybe it was Ridge, tired of their feud. Maybe he was calling her to join him on his walk. She gave a hiss of disappointment when she saw that the call had nothing to do with Ridge at all. It was Aurelio.

"Hi, Aurelio," Lani said, trying her best to sound cheerful but not doing a good job at it.

"Hello, Doctor. I call to wish you safe travel back to the United States."

"Oh, thank you. That's sweet of you." If Lani were perfectly honest she would say, after she'd paid the guide the balance of his fee, she hadn't expected to hear from him again. His call was truly a pleasant surprise.

"But you do not sound very happy, Doctor. I know why."

Lani rolled her eyes. Yeah, he would know, all right. He'd been there to witness the not-too-subtle quarrel between her and Ridge and the silent war that raged between them all the way back to the city. She was just surprised he'd actually brought it up.

"And I know what you must do." There was an enigmatic quality to Aurelio's voice.

That made Lani curious. "You do?"

"Yes. You must rock the boat, throw it off balance. You must do the unexpected."

Now what was that supposed to mean? "Ookaay." Lani dragged out the word, trying to decipher the meaning behind the old man's cryptic statement.

Before she could ask him to clarify he spoke again. "I will say no more. Now I bid you a good evening and a good trip back to America."

Long after Aurelio had hung up Lani sat there, thinking on his words. Rock the boat, he'd said. In short, do something surprising. She was good with surprises. She could do this.

And just like that an idea came to her. But could she pull it off before Ridge got back?

Quickly, she grabbed the hotel phone and asked to be connected with the restaurant manager.

"Yes," he said, "we can do that but not before seven o'clock."

Lani glanced at the clock. Six-eighteen. Ridge would be back by then. She hoped. "Great," she said. "Go ahead and book them for me."

As soon as she hung up the phone she dashed into the bathroom. She wanted to be ready. There was not a moment to lose. Twenty minutes later she was dressed in a midnight-blue cocktail dress, an outfit that always made her hair look its blackest and shiniest. She was wearing her dangly earrings that accentuated her slender neck and she'd decided to wear make-up – one of her rare moments, but tonight she wanted to look super-special for him.

And not a moment too soon. At sixteen minutes before seven the door to the hotel suite opened and Ridge walked in. When he saw her he froze. Then his eyebrows raised and he gave a low whistle. "You look sensational. What's the special occasion?"

From the other side of the living room she smiled and gave a little shrug. "Oh, nothing much. Just a little...engagement. There's a gentleman I know, I'm supposed to meet him tonight for dinner."

Ridge's brows fell. "What gentleman? You didn't tell me you were going out to dinner."

"Oh, it was sort of...sudden. An impromptu arrangement, you could say."

"Oh." Ridge's face was now so dark it was thunderous. "Let me not keep you, then." Not sparing her another glance he marched off to the bathroom.

Lani grinned. So far so good. If all went well he would be good and well-roasted in his rage by the time the seven o'clock hour came around.

She heard when Ridge exited the bathroom but then he took a long time in the bedroom, probably stewing over her words while he dressed. Lani didn't mind because by the time he came back into the living room all would be ready.

True to the manager's word, at one minute before the seven o'clock deadline she heard a tap at the door. She rushed over and opened to a black-suited, bow tied man pushing a dinner trolley laden with the most sumptuous fare anyone could want – wild Norwegian salmon in cream sauce, filet mignon with baby carrots and potatoes and chicken cordon bleu. There was also a dish which the manager had called 'Chef's Surprise'. She had no idea what it was and she hadn't bothered to ask.

Lani directed the server to the dining table she'd decorated with softly-burning candles and a bouquet of tropical flowers and there he laid out the dishes, filling the air with a mouth-watering aroma.

As he straightened and turned to push the trolley away Lani raised her eyebrows. "The rest of your crew?" she whispered.

He smiled. "They were instructed to come up fifteen minutes after the hour to give you time to settle down."

"Okay. That makes sense." She rubbed her hands together. Things would be perfect if Ridge would leave the bedroom just as soon as the server left. He would be surprised by the romantic dinner she'd arranged which would put him in a mellow mood before she executed part two of her plan. With that thought in mind she gave the man a hearty tip then quickly rushed him and his dinner trolley out the door and turned off all the lights in the room. The only illumination was the soft glow from the candles.

With everything in place, Lani went to sit at the table and wait for her husband to appear. Five minutes passed but there was no Ridge, which made Lani frown. What was taking him so long? She didn't want the food to get cold. After another two minutes she decided to go check on him. She found him sprawled out on top of the bed in nothing but his boxer shorts. He was lying on his back, arms folded across her chest. He was staring up at the ceiling, a dark scowl on his face.

"What are you doing?" she asked, stepping into the room. "Aren't you going to get dressed?"

"For what?" he growled. "It's not like I'm going anywhere." Then his glare left the ceiling and he trained it on her. "Who's this guy you're going out with? And why the heck did you set up this date? You're my wife." His eyes narrowed. "Or did you forget that part?"

Ridge was really jealous now, which was the effect Lani had been going for. The more riled up she got him the hotter their lovemaking would be once she'd wined and dined him. At least, that was her theory.

If she ever got a chance to do the wining and dining... He looked like he'd taken up permanent residence right there in the middle of the bed. She decided to try another tactic. "I have a surprise for you. Why don't you get dressed and come out to the living room?"

He gave her a suspicious glare. "I'm not interested."

"Oh, come on," she said, exasperated. "Stop being so stubborn. You know you want to see what it is."

"Actually, I don't." He gave her a cool look. "If you want to get me out there so you can introduce me to your date, it ain't happening."

"Will you stop being an ass and get yourself into the living room?" Lani gave a hiss of annoyance and turned toward the door. There was just so much patience she could exercise. "You get your butt outside, do you hear me? You have two minutes."

With that she stalked off to plop herself back into her chair at the dining table. She was mad. After she'd gone to all this trouble her fabulous dinner was getting cold and it was all because of that obstinate, unreasonable man. She folded her arms across her chest, gritted her teeth and waited. She would give him two minutes and no more.

But after two minutes there was no sign of Ridge. Lani let out an exasperated sigh but she kept her bottom glued to the chair. She was not going to run after Ridge. She sat there, refusing to look at the clock, and she waited and waited. And still no Ridge.

Finally, no longer able to resist, she looked up at the clock on the wall. Seven-sixteen. Ridge had kept her waiting over ten minutes and on top of that the cursed musicians were late.

The tap at the door came just on the tail end of that thought, just when she'd decided she didn't want any damn music, anyway. But when she opened the door there they were, three of them, and they were grinning from ear to ear.

Lani gave them the less than welcoming greeting of a groan. "Is it too late to cancel you guys?"

"Yup," the short one said and before she could even think of closing the door he walked in, his two tuxedoed buddies behind him.

It seemed that things were out of her hands. She was about to be serenaded, whether she wanted it or not.

With a sigh of resignation she went back to the table and sat. Talk about a waste of time. But she'd ordered them so she guessed she would just have to sit through it. Alone.

"Ready, madam?" the one who looked like the leader asked.

Lani grimaced. "Yeah. Go ahead."

***

What the heck? Was somebody holding a concert in the living room?

Although Ridge's scowl had disappeared long ago, now it came back full force. There were violins playing in the living room and he had no idea why.

He gave a grunt of annoyance. Lani must be desperate, resorting to playing classical music to get him to leave the bedroom. Well, it wasn't going to work.

But then the music got louder, almost sounding like it was live. But it couldn't be.

His curiosity getting the better of him, Ridge got up off the bed and padded across the floor to throw the bedroom door open. What he saw made him draw back in surprise.

Three violinists stood around Lani where she sat at the dining table and they were playing with such concentration and feeling you would think they were performing in front of an audience of a thousand.

And there was Lani, sitting at the table laden with dish upon dish, and she had her head down and it looked like she was...crying?

He'd made a couple of steps forward when she looked up, her eyes widening as she saw him. "Ridge," she gasped. "You're not dressed."

He looked down and saw that she was right. He'd walked out into the living room in nothing but his boxer shorts. But how could he have known she had real live musicians performing in their hotel suite?

But when the men saw him they did not pause in their serenade. True professionals, they swung their attention back to the woman at the table and continued playing.

So this was the surprise Lani had spoken about. She'd arranged dinner and music for them. And, he now realized, the man with whom she'd planned on having dinner, was him.

That knowledge made him feel like the biggest jerk there was. His main concern the beautiful woman sitting at the table, Ridge strode toward her, not even bothered by his near naked state. He had other, far more important things to think about like how to get back into the good graces of his wife. As soon as he got to her side he went to drop to his knees, ready to shower her with apologies, but before he could do it she pulled him down and practically shoved him into the chair beside her.

Before he could move, before he could even speak, she'd left her chair and was climbing onto his lap, the tears sliding down her cheeks to fall onto his bare chest. "I'm sorry, Ridge. It's my fault we're not speaking. All my fault."

Ridge lifted his arms to gather her close but then the violin music and the ready-made audience got to him. He looked up at the men of music who were performing like mad even though their ears were obviously cocked to hear what would come next.

Ridge cleared his throat. "Thanks, guys," he told them. "You've done a great job. You may go now."

Abruptly, they stopped playing then one of them had the audacity to make his disappointment obvious. "Aaw," he said, dropping his violin from where he'd hooked it on his shoulder. "We were just getting to the good part."

Ridge couldn't tell if he meant the good part of the musical piece or of the scene unfolding before his eyes. Whichever it was, the show was over. He jerked his chin toward the door. "Please show yourselves out."

They couldn't leave fast enough as far as Ridge was concerned. As soon as the door closed behind them he looked down at the woman in his arms. "What were you saying now, honey?"

Lani was calmer now and she snuggled in his lap and leaned her cheek against his chest. "I was telling you how awful I was."

Ridge chuckled. "We both know that's not true. You're the sweetest girl in the world."

Instead of thanking him for the compliment Lani gave him an irritated look and swatted him on the shoulder. "That sounded so corny," she said crossly.

He shrugged. "What can I say? It's true."

She dropped her head back to his chest and wrapped her arms around his waist. "Anyway, I was telling you I was a stupid jerk for not telling you what really happened when Aurelio and I went on our hike."

Ridge frowned, his arms tightening around her. "Something happened?"

She nodded, her hair rubbing against his skin as she moved her head. "I was too embarrassed to tell you. I was scared you'd get mad at me."

"What happened out there, Lani?" Ridge's heart was picking up pace. No matter that she was safe in his arms, just the thought that she might have been in danger made the hair on his arms stand on end.

Lani gave a sigh that made her sound exhausted. "We got lost. That's why we got back to camp so late. We'd been walking in circles for hours. I was so scared to tell you. That's why I played cool, like you were making a big deal out of nothing. But it really was a big deal. We could have been stuck out there all night." She shivered and snuggled closer, like the memory had taken her back to that place and time when she'd been at the mercy of the wild jungle.

His heart going out to her, imagining the degree of her fear, he dipped his head to give her a reassuring kiss on the forehead. "Oh, honey, you should have told me. I would have understood. You don't know how I almost went crazy, not knowing where you were. I was so relieved when you walked back into camp. You have no idea."

Lani nodded. "I know you were worried. I could see that. I just...I guess the shock of it all just made me act crazy." Then she pulled back from him and peered up into his face. "When we got back you weren't in the tent. What were you doing in the bushes?"

"I was just setting off. I was going to look for you."

Lani's brows lifted. "You were going to head out into the jungle in the dark and trek eight miles with only one leg?"

He smiled. "One leg and a half."

She did not look amused. "Are you crazy?"

His smile deepened. "Crazy for you, my love. Only for you."

It seemed he'd said the perfect words because the pout on her lips disappeared and she smiled and sank back against him. "Do you know what I'm happiest about?" she asked.

"No," he whispered in her ear. "What?"

"That you blackmailed me into marrying you. It's the best thing that could have happened to me." She gave a soft, contented sigh.

"Are you sure, my sweet? You don't want to get me for playing that dirty trick on you?" Ridge was smiling but this time he was one hundred percent serious. He had to know – had his wife fallen in love with him? Had she fallen under the spell that had bewitched him from the first day he laid eyes on her?

"Oh, I'm going to get you, all right. I can't let an inveterate trickster go unpunished." Then, as if to soften the scare she'd just put in him, she pulled his head down and kissed the tip of his nose. "But don't worry," she said softly. "When I get you back it won't hurt at all. You made me love you too much." And then she cupped his face in her hands and drew him down until their lips touched and Lani gave him a kiss full of such promise that he knew it was going to be a long night.

And he didn't mind at all.

EPILOGUE

"Oh, my dear. I'm so proud of you." Marie had tears in her eyes as she leaned over to give Lani a kiss on the cheek.

"And so am I. Great work." Her father patted her on the hand.

Lani smiled. "Thanks Mom, Dad." But then she looked across the banquet table at the man who had made it all possible. "And thank you, Ridge," she said, her voice loud and clear and trembling with pride, "for making this dream come true."

Never one to make a big deal about all the good he was doing, Ridge just smiled back and gave her a wink. And she knew exactly what that meant. Later, when they were home and alone, she would have to pay him back, not in cash, but in kind – the kind of 'kind' she really, really liked.

But Lani had to kill that naughty thought because now she was being called to the platform. As her family and her colleagues from the scientific community warmed her spirit with their applause, she made her way to the front of the room and went to receive her award.

"Leilani Kent, in recognition of your stellar work and your contribution to research in the area of neurodegenerative diseases, we present you with the Antioch Award of Excellence."

The applause rose and the crowd cheered and Lani felt the tears prick the corners of her eyes. She could not have been more proud. Like she was one of the winners at the Academy Awards she held her trophy high, her eyes glued on Ridge and then, as he nodded with pride, she blew him a kiss.

Later that night, as everyone gathered in the lobby to say their goodbyes, Lani drew her mother away from the crowd.

"I have something to tell you," she whispered in Marie's ear.

"What is it, dear? You're not going away on another of your South America trips, are you?"

Lani shook her head. "No. Even better. I won't be doing overseas trips for a while. And that's what I want to tell you. You finally got your wish."

"My wish? Whatever do you mean?"

"You're going to be a grandmother. I'm having a baby."

"Oh, oh!" Marie's eyes grew wide and she slapped her hand over her heart. "You're pregnant?"

Lani nodded. "Four months. Get yourself ready. You'll soon have your hands full with Baby Kent."

"Oh, oh." Marie was clutching her chest now.

Startled by her mother's gasps, Lani's eyes widened and she grabbed Marie's arm. "Mom, are you all right?"

"Am I?" Marie said. "You've just made me the happiest woman in the world."

Relief washing through her, Lani could only smile. Her mother couldn't know it, but someone else had already seized that title. Because, Lani knew, no woman in the world could be happier than she.

But she wouldn't tell her mother that. Why burst her bubble?

As happy as she was, it was a title Lani was more than willing to share.

Thank you for reading!

<u>Free book offer:</u> Get your free copy of 'Rome for the Holidays' by joining my mailing list. On signing up you will be provided with the link to the story. Just visit my website to join:

<u>www.judyangelo.com</u>[1]

If you've already read this story and would simply like notification when I have new books out, still visit my website and click on the sign-up link to join my mailing list. You may then choose to ignore the link to the free book. When new stories are out I'll keep you posted.

<u>www.judyangelo.com</u>[2]

If you wish to drop me a line, please send your e-mail to:
<u>judyangeloauthor@gmail.com</u>

I would love to hear from you!

---

1. http://www.judyangelo.com/

2. http://www.judyangelo.com/

Sneak Preview for the next in the series:
THE BILLIONAIRE BROTHERS KENT
Book 4

Bossing the Billionaire
CHAPTER ONE

"Where the heck am I?" Ryder muttered the words under his breath as he stared at the stretch of deserted road ahead of him.

So much for taking the scenic route. He'd gotten so sick of the dreary monotony of the highway that he'd taken a detour, deciding to try some of the country roads instead. Now, in hindsight, it seemed it hadn't been such a good plan after all, especially considering that he had no idea where in the world he was right now.

"What kind of a GPS are you?" he grumbled to the device set in the middle of the dashboard but it only stared back at him, mute and blank-faced. Ryder gave it a disgusted glare. "Not much of a help, are you?"

The thing was, before Ryder took to the country roads he'd known he would sort of be on his own for some parts of the journey. There were some roads that the GPS hadn't been programmed for. But jeez, he'd expected the device to pick up most of them, not leave him stranded in the middle of nowhere. At the thought, he had to bite back another grumble.

For this part of his journey Ryder was on his way to Marfa, a tiny town he'd heard about at his last stop in Fort Stockton. What he heard piqued his interest and since he didn't mind prolonging his road trip he decided to make a stop there. The directions they'd given him at the rest stop had seemed pretty straightforward...until now that he was over an hour into the journey and with no town in sight and with no hope of getting cell phone service way out in this wilderness. He hadn't seen another living soul since he'd turned onto the road. God help him if he ran out of gas. The hyenas would gladly have him for lunch.

It was another half hour before Ryder saw what looked like a tiny settlement up ahead. "There is a God," he muttered under his breath even as he let out a relieved sigh.

In minutes he was rolling into a tiny service station-cum-convenience store. As soon as he pulled in, a stout man in checkered shirt and jeans hurried over. "What's for you, stranger? Need to fill 'er up?"

The man gave him a smile so wide Ryder couldn't help but smile back. "I'd appreciate that," he said as he climbed out of his truck. "You guys take credit cards, right?"

"I ain't too sure about that," the man said with a shrug. "I don't work here."

That made Ryder raise his eyebrows in surprise. Was the fellow so friendly he would offer to pump gas for a stranger? Or maybe he was after a tip. Ryder had no problem with that. He always had loose bills in his pocket for pretty much that purpose. He was no stranger to people doing whatever odd thing they could to make a buck or two on the street.

Still grinning, the man jerked his head toward the glass door to the convenience store. "Go on in," he said as he reached for the pump. "You can ask about the credit card thing inside."

"Will do." Ryder nodded and left him to his task. He walked across the asphalted pavement and pulled the door open. He was immediately hit by a gust of warm, stale air. He jerked back, holding the door open a while longer to let some of the outdoor air in. Hadn't these people heard about something called air conditioning? This was Texas in the middle of July, for Pete's sake.

He stepped inside but, momentarily blinded by the dimness, he had to blink to reorient his eyes. It took a few seconds before he saw the wizened old man sitting behind the counter, his eyes glued to a newspaper spread out in front of him. Even when the bell tinkled as the door opened and closed the white-haired man did not look up.

Ryder cleared his throat. Even so, the old geezer – for want of a better description – continued to ignore him.

He cleared his throat again then seeing that wasn't working he stepped forward and slapped his hand down on the counter.

The old man jumped. His head jerked up and he glared at Ryder. "Hey, where did you come from? What's with you, young fella, sneaking up on a man like that? You nigh gave me a heart attack." He jerked the newspaper away then folded it up, even as he continued to scowl.

"I'm sorry," Ryder said. "I wanted to ask you a question."

"Say what? You've got to speak up, fella. What's with a big, strapping one like you whispering at me like that?" Clearly annoyed, the man threw his newspaper down and got up off his stool. "Come on, speak up."

"I said I need to ask you a question." Ryder raised his voice another decibel for the benefit of the man.

"So ask it. What's stopping you?"

"Do you take credit cards?"

"Credit what? You joshin' me or what? We don't give no credit at this here establishment. Credit got run out of town nigh on fifty years ago."

"I didn't ask you for credit. I asked if you take credit cards."

"And what did I tell ya? Are you deaf? No credit. Strictly cash at my establishment." The man was leaning forward now, looking like he was getting ready to throw Ryder out.

"Not very friendly, are you?" Ryder knew his muttered statement had no chance of being heard, not by this one who was obviously as deaf as a doorpost. This man was the exact opposite of the one he'd met outside. He reached into his back pocket and pulled out his wallet. "No problem," he said. "I've got cash. How much do I owe you for gas?" He'd seen when his friendly helper had rested the hose back in its cradle so he knew the tank was full.

"How should I know?" the storekeeper asked as he slid off his stool and lifted a section of the counter top. "I have to go out and see."

One would have expected the man to see the total on a computer screen inside the store but Ryder didn't bother to question that. He simply stepped back and let this not-so-pleasant business operator walk past.

Within a minute he was back. "You owe me fifty-five forty-five," he said as he stepped past Ryder to retake his post behind the counter. "Strictly cash."

"I hear you." Ryder took out three twenty-dollar bills and laid them on the counter. "Keep the change."

Old Mr. Grumpy must have liked the sound of that because his face brightened and for the first time since he laid eyes on the man Ryder saw him smile. "Hey there, fella. Now you're the kind of man I like to do business with. Not like them noisy whippersnappers who come riding through here on their motorbikes."

Ryder almost smiled. So that was it. The old fellow must have thought he was one of 'them'. He'd probably been harassed by some young, crazy teenagers riding through the place – although what teenagers on motorbikes would be doing all the way out here in the boondocks, Ryder couldn't tell. Still, the fact that the old man put him in the same category was downright amusing. At three decades plus one year he was way, way past the teenager stage.

"So where're you from?" the man asked, suddenly looking like he was ready for conversation. "I know you ain't from around these parts."

Ryder didn't return the smile. He would answer the questions but the man's cool reception had been a real turn-off. "I'm from Des Moines," he said, and left it at that.

"Ah ha. An Iowa man." The storeowner nodded. "And what are you doing in this part of Texas? It ain't like this is Dallas or Houston."

"I'm on my way to a town called Marfa. I heard about it at my last stop in Fort Stockton, that there's this phenomenon that takes place at night. The Marfa lights in the sky. Nobody can explain it." He shrugged. "I always was a sucker for a good mystery so I'm on my way to this Marfa place. Is it anywhere near here?"

The man chuckled. "You're standing in the middle of it, young fella." He stuck his hand out. "The name's Simeon. Simeon Harris. Ask me anything you want to know about Marfa. Been living here all my life."

Ryder took his hand but as he did he was frowning. "This is Marfa? This deserted one-storey sha...establishment?" He'd been about to say shack but he stopped himself just in time.

"Yup," the man said, beaming, but then his grin turned sheepish. "To tell the truth, this ain't quite the middle. It's just the outskirts but it's one of the first establishments in this here town. Was built long before the town grew so big. Almost two thousand of us now, you know."

Ryder looked back at him, confused. "So where are the rest of you? Outside of your...establishment...all I'm seeing is wide open plains and tumbleweed."

He grinned. "Oh, they're still a ways in. The newer part of the city's where they all hang out but me, I like it right where I am. I pick up the strays before they run out of gas." And although he didn't say it, the way he was looking at Ryder told him he'd just been put in the stray category. "That's how I make my dough."

"So how do I get to Marfa?" Ryder asked. "The city part, I mean."

"Well, you just head-"

"It's okay, old Sim. I'll direct him." They both turned as the helper stepped into the already tight space. "I'll make sure ye get there all right."

"Well, okay," Ryder said then he turned back to Simeon and gave him a nod. "Thank you."

"And thank you," Simeon said. "Come back any time."

Ryder was surprised when, as they stepped out of the tiny convenience store, the helpful one stepped closer and gave him a not-too-gentle pat on the shoulder. "There's something about you," he said. "I don't know what it is but old Simeon likes you. I can see that much." Then, his hand still on Ryder's shoulder, he turned him to face west. "Now you see that post way over there? You take the road and go past it and you're going to take a road branching off to the right. It will take you a little ways down but never you mind that. Just keep going until you run into the sign that says Marfa."

"So I'll see a sign?"

"You'll see a sign. Can't miss it," he assured Ryder. "And like I said, if you don't see nobody for a while don't be alarmed. It's still a little ways off."

"Okay. I appreciate you telling me that." Ryder dug into his pocket and pulled out some bills. "Thanks a lot for your help."

The man's smile widened. "No problem," he said with a nod. "No problem at all."

Even when Ryder jumped into the Dodge Ram and drove off the man still stood there, staring after the truck and grinning.

As he watched the man through the rearview mirror Ryder shook his head. "Weird," he said under his breath. They were both weird, the grumpy old man and the overly friendly one. From two opposite poles, they were. He could only wonder if the other residents of Marfa would be just as unusual.

Ryder had been driving for the better part of half an hour when he began to wonder if he'd taken a wrong turn. Texas was known for its wide-open spaces but he'd expected to be in Marfa long before this. He'd followed his guide's instructions to the letter but there was still no sign welcoming him to Marfa. Where the heck was the place?

So the man had said it was some way away – aways off as he'd put it – and not to panic if he didn't see the place right away, but instead of getting wider the road was narrowing and on top of that it was getting bumpier by the mile. There was no way there could be a city at the end of this road.

Not knowing if it made sense to turn back at that point, he drove on. He'd been at it for another ten minutes when the bumpy asphalted surface got even worse. Now it was nothing but a dirt road. What the heck?

Ryder slammed on the brakes. "You've got to be kidding me." He let out his breath in a hiss. Had he taken a wrong turn? Or had he been taken for a ride?

And then he saw it. Off in the distance, the golden rays of the setting sun to the back of it, was a building visible only because it was all of two stories high. At least that was what it looked like from this distance. For the second time that day Ryder had to breathe a sigh of relief. Not a moment too soon. He'd been just about ready to turn around and head back the way he'd come. Now, finally, he'd found Marfa. There wasn't much to it, just one building that he could see so far, but he would take it. He was too exhausted to feel anything but glad to see this sign of life in the middle of the Texas desert plains.

He pressed on the gas and shot up the dirt road toward the safe haven. There was still no sign saying 'Welcome to Marfa' but he didn't care as long as there was food and a warm bed up ahead.

It was when he got closer that he saw how sparse the place really was. Outside of the building he'd spotted he was now seeing another six or seven but they were all tiny and all looking in dire need of repairs. Was this the Marfa he'd been hearing about? He'd been expecting some improvement on the gas station he'd left behind but this place actually looked worse. He hadn't thought that could be possible.

As he approached the main building he slowed down and when he pulled up close by he read the words painted on the front. Beaumont's. That was all it said and even as he got out of the truck he had no idea what kind of place it was.

With a tired sigh he slammed the door shut behind him and trudged up the dusty path that led to the front entrance. As he walked he noticed a truck parked in back, then two. Maybe that was the parking area but it didn't matter. Right then he was too tired and hungry to go back and move his truck. He just wanted some grub.

Ryder pushed the front door open and, like at the gas station, there was the sound of a bell tinkling above. The lighting in the room wasn't great but he could plainly see the half a dozen men who turned at his entrance. They were lounging around tables, each man with a drink in his hand. That was when Ryder realized he'd stumbled on some kind of bar.

"Howdy, stranger," one of the men said, holding up his mug of beer. "Pull up a chair." The way he said the word made it sound like 'cheer'.

"Uh, thanks," Ryder said, letting the door close behind him, but he didn't move, still taken aback by the unexpected invitation. These Texans were something else. They were either super-friendly or downright crabby. Was there no middle ground with these people?

"Go on. He's not going to bite."

At the sound of a female voice, a bright and bold, almost teasing tone, Ryder's head jerked up and he found himself locking gaze with the most startling ebony eyes he'd ever seen. It wasn't so much the color of the eyes that got him but the audacious stare she'd fixed on him. Like a goddess who deigned to associate with mere mortals, the look she gave Ryder told him that in this little part of the planet she was the woman in charge.

And if that wasn't enough to make him stand rooted to the spot, on top of that the woman was breathtakingly beautiful. A mass of wavy, dark hair tumbled over her shoulders, framing a face blessed with high cheekbones, a pert nose and the sexiest lips he'd been ever so lucky to behold. She was the lone flower in a field of pot bellied beer-drinking men and among such weeds her beauty bloomed brilliant. And she knew it. He could see it in the way she carried herself, back straight and eyes fearless as she stared at him.

The beauty leaned forward to rest her elbows on the bar counter and her luscious lips curved into a smile. "Are you going to stand there staring at me the whole evening?" she asked, tilting her head as she regarded him with amusement. "Your butt got something against chairs?"

Ryder blinked. He'd thought he had a good handle on women but this one took him by surprise. When it came to being shy or reserved this girl didn't know the meaning of the words. But how a woman so young could be so bold in a sea full of grizzly men, he couldn't figure out. Instead of being intimidated it looked like she was the one who usually did the intimidating.

Before she could throw out a command Ryder cleared his throat and tore his eyes away from the mesmerizing Texas rose then he glanced down at the man who had invited him over. His unexpected host was still grinning up at him so he figured the invitation was still open. With a shrug he headed over to the table where the man sat with another, a smaller man, who stared up at him in open curiosity.

As he approached, the big man used his foot to push the free chair away from the table. "Make yourself comfortable, stranger. It's not everyday we see a new face in these parts."

Ryder gave him a nod of appreciation for the welcome. "Thank you," he said as he took the seat that was being offered. "This is my first visit to Marfa."

"Marfa?" The bearded man let out a hearty guffaw. "Did you hear that, fellas? This stranger thinks he's in Marfa."

The man got the reaction he'd probably been looking for. The whole place erupted in raucous laughter and, to Ryder's chagrin, even the woman behind the bar was chuckling.

Feeling like a fool, he cleared his throat again then frowned when he realized he'd fallen right back into his nervous habit. Whenever he felt out of his depth he was always clearing his throat. It was a habit he'd thought he'd licked but now it was back, just when he didn't need it causing him even further embarrassment.

"Where am I then?" he asked, now giving up hope of ever finding this place called Marfa.

"This is Pequoia," the woman said as the laughter died down. "One of the oldest towns in Texas." Then she gave him a rueful grin. "Now one of the smallest, what with all the youngsters leaving as soon as they're old enough." Then she dried her hands on a nearby towel, lifted the counter and came over to him, a letter-sized laminated card in her hand. "Here's the menu. You might as well make yourself comfortable and grab a bite. Looks like you've been on the road a while."

Ryder gladly took it from her hand but it wasn't the food list that held his attention. It was her. She was even lovelier close up.

"What did I tell you about staring?" Her voice was brusque but her lips twitched then curved into a crooked smile that had Ryder smiling back.

"Sorry." Suitably chastised he glanced down at the menu. "The roast beef sandwich sounds good. Can I have that?"

"It's your lucky day," she said. "That's the most popular item on the menu but it so happens I've got some left. Just enough for one."

"I'll take it," Ryder said, his mouth already watering at the thought of the meal. He hadn't eaten since breakfast and at this hour of the day he'd reached starvation point.

The woman nodded and took the menu from his hand and was just about to turn away when Ryder stopped her. "Do you mind if I ask your name?"

She stopped and actually looked surprised that he'd asked. "It's Blake. Blake Beaumont. And what's yours, stranger?"

"I'm Ryder Kent." He put out his hand. "I'm pleased to meet you, Blake."

She took it even as she cocked an eyebrow at him, the amusement back in her eyes. "Are you sure about that? Maybe you should get to know me better before you throw out such statements."

"Yeah," one of the men from a neighboring table said. "This is one tough gal, my friend. Don't be fooled by all this beauty. When she's ready she can be a real b-"

"Calvin, you mind your mouth, you hear me?" Blake's voice was stern. "No need to scare off Mr. Kent with your crude language."

"Call me Ryder," he began but she'd already turned away and was heading back to the bar. Well, so much for striking up a conversation with the sole woman in the place. He might as well turn his attention to his new-found friends.

Within minutes of a lively conversation about the current issues plaguing the dairy industry Blake was back with a salad and the sandwich that smelled so good it made Ryder's stomach growl.

She smiled. "I could tell you were hungry. It's all yours. Chow down." She laid the plate on the table then handed him his silverware rapped in a white cloth napkin.

He glanced across at his table companions. "May I order something for you gentlemen?" He hoped they'd say yes. It was going to feel weird, chomping on his sandwich while they just sat there and watched.

"We already ate," the small man said.

"But I'm all out of beer," the big one said. "I could do with another one, for the road."

Somebody behind Ryder cleared his throat, a not-too-subtle hint that a drink would be welcome at that table, too.

Ryder grinned. It seemed they were all too eager to take advantage of a generous offer and he didn't mind at all. "Drinks on the house," he said, loud enough for Blake to hear. "It's on me."

She heard all right. Before he'd taken his second bite she'd come from behind the counter, a tray of drinks in hand. She obviously knew what each of her patrons drank because she didn't ask a single one for his order. She just served.

"And what about you, Ryder?" she asked, pausing at his table. "What are you having?"

"I'll just take some cranberry juice," he said, "if you have any."

"Sure do." And then, as if this was the sort of thing you did in a place like this, she gave a man at a neighboring table a quick cuff to the back of the head. "Stop snickering and drink your beer."

Ryder almost snorted in laughter but his mouth was full. Obviously, Blake Beaumont was not one to trifle with.

A half hour passed and then an hour and by that time most of the men had left, leaving only the two at Ryder's table. The darkness of night was now properly settled on the land and he could feel the exhaustion creeping up on him. Time to get going.

He lifted a hand to catch Blake's attention. "Could I have the bill, please?"

She tore her eyes away from the small T.V set in the corner of the room. She'd been absorbed in the T.V news for the past half hour but she picked up a piece of paper from the counter and walked over. "Here you go," she said, depositing the bill on the table in front of him. "You racked up a pretty hefty bill, buying all those rounds of drinks. You'd better be good for it."

"Don't worry," he said, grinning up at her. "I am." Little did she know he could buy all the drinks she could ever serve. Heck, he could buy the whole town, and more. Still smiling, Ryder reached around to dig his wallet out of his back pocket.

His hand slid in and came back out...empty. "Sorry." He gave her an embarrassed grin and dug into the other back pocket. Nothing. He frowned. "Weird." As he muttered the word he shoved a hand into the front pocket on the left then the one on the right. His frown deepening, he patted the pocket of the denim jacket he was wearing. Still nothing.

Ryder cleared his throat. "I'm sorry. It looks like I left my wallet in the truck. I'll have to go get it."

Before he'd gotten all the words out Blake's smile had disappeared and in its place was a glare that said she was not amused. "Do you really think I'm going to fall for that? You're trying to pull a fast one on me, aren't you?"

Ryder shook his head. "No, I'm not. I swear. My wallet must have fallen out in the truck. I'll just go get it and come right back."

Blake gave him a look of suspicion and then she looked at the big man sitting at Ryder's table. "Go with him, Ted. Make sure he doesn't try to take off."

"You got it." Ted was grinning as he got up then he cracked the knuckles on his beefy hands. "Come on, buster. Let's go see if you can put your money where your mouth is."

Ryder shrugged. "I've got no problem with that." He got up and walked in front of Ted, out the door and toward the Dodge Ram. He pulled the door open and glanced at the driver's seat then the passenger's seat. He didn't see anything so he checked if it had fallen between the seats or onto the floor. It was nowhere in sight.

As he pulled back and straightened up Ted grinned at him. "You really were pulling a fast one. You think you're slick, don't you?"

Ryder felt like punching the jeering smile off his lips. "I'm not pulling anything. I must have dropped my wallet somewhere. It's okay. I'll call..." As the last word left his lips he realized something. He'd gone through his pocket and his truck and he hadn't run into his cell phone at all. That was missing, too.

"Oh, shoot." The words left his lips in a groan of realization. "That guy at the gas station. How could I have been so stupid? I should have known he was too darned friendly to be real."

Ted gave a snort of derision. "Don't tell me you're going to draw for some story about getting robbed."

"But it's true. My wallet and my cell phone are gone."

Ryder's words were like the signal for Ted to get rough. The man clamped a massive hand around his upper arm, his lips curling in a sneer. "Come on, bud," he snarled. "You ain't going to cheat the little lady out of her dough. You're coming with me."

Ryder didn't even bother to resist. Talk about embarrassing.

He was not looking forward to explaining himself to Miss Blake Beaumont.

Click here to get your copy of 'Bossing the Billionaire' from your favorite online retailer.

BAD BOY BILLIONAIRES
Volume 1 - Tamed by the Billionaire
Volume 2 - Maid in the USA
Volume 3 - Billionaire's Island Bride
Volume 4 - Dangerous Deception
Volume 5 - To Tame a Tycoon
Volume 6 - Sweet Seduction
Volume 7 - Daddy by December
Volume 8 - To Catch a Man (in 30 Days or Less)
Volume 9 – Bedding her Billionaire Boss
Volume 10 - Her Indecent Proposal
Volume 11 - So Much Trouble When She Walked In
Volume 12 – Married by Midnight

THE BILLIONAIRE BROTHERS KENT
Book 1 - The Billionaire Next Door
Book 2 - Babies for the Billionaire
Book 3 - Billionaire's Blackmail Bride
Book 4 - Bossing the Billionaire

THE CASTILLOS
Book 1 - Beauty and the Beastly Billionaire
Book 2 – Training the Tycoon
Book 3 – The Mogul's Maiden Mistress
Book 4 – Eva and the Extreme Executive

HOLIDAY EDITIONS
Rome for the Holidays (Novella)
Rome for Always (Novel)

The NAUGHTY AND NICE Series
Volume 1 - **Naughty by Nature**

COMEDY, CONFLICT & ROMANCE Series
Book 1 - Taming the Fury
Book 2 - Outwitting the Wolf
Book 3 – Romancing Malone

COLLECTIONS
BAD BOY BILLIONAIRES, Coll. I - Vols. 1 - 4
BAD BOY BILLIONAIRES, Coll. II - Vols. 5 - 8
BAD BOY BILLIONAIRES, Coll. III - Vols. 9 - 12
BILLIONAIRE BROS. KENT - Books 1 - 4

Author contact:
www.judyangelo.com[1]
judyangeloauthor@gmail.com

---

1. http://www.judyangelo.com/

Copyright © 2014 Judy Angelo
Phoenix Publishing Limited

This book is a work of fiction. The names, characters, places, and incidents are products of the writer's imagination or have been used fictitiously. Any resemblance to persons, living or dead, is entirely coincidental.

Author contact:
judyangeloauthor@gmail.com

Connect with me on Facebook:
Judy Angelo Author[2]

Cover Artist: Ramona Lockwood (Covers by Ramona)

---

2. https://www.facebook.com/pages/Judy-Angelo-Author/207657399403357?ref=hl

Did you love *Billionaire's Blackmail Bride*? Then you should read *Tamed by the Billionaire (Roman's Story)*[3] by JUDY ANGELO!

THE TAMING OF A PRINCESS...

Serena Van Buren, the privileged daughter of a wealthy businessman, can't wait to begin her three-month tour of Europe with her college mates. Little does she know that fate has other plans in store! Instead of dancing with handsome Italians and dining with charming Frenchmen Serena finds herself trapped in a six-month internship with overbearing business tycoon, Roman Steele - an arrangement orchestrated by her own father.

Serena is determined to show Roman that she won't yield to the demands of any man, boss or no boss. She's a Van Buren, after all, known to wither a man with one look. But Roman Steele is like no

---

3. https://books2read.com/u/4EQ1l4

4. https://books2read.com/u/4EQ1l4

man she's ever met before. Suave, sexy and stunningly handsome, there's something about him that she can't resist. It looks like Serena Van Buren has finally met her match.

A sweet and saucy romance that will have you smiling...

Read more at judyangelo.blogspot.com.

Also by JUDY ANGELO

Bad Boy Billionaires - Where Are They Now?
Tamed by the Billionaire - The Sequel

Billionaire Bachelorettes of Bel-Air
In Bed with the Enemy

Billionaire Brotherhood
The Billionaire Brotherhood III, Vols. 9 - 12

Historias Multimillionarias para Navidad
Rome para Navidad

KNOWLEDGE in a NUTSHELL
How to Write a Romance Novel

MADE FOR THE MOVIES Fantasy Romance
Trading Spaces
Back from the Future
Back from the Future with BONUS Trading Spaces

Multimillonarios Machos
Domada por el Multimillionario
Domado por el Multimillionario, Bilingual Version

The BAD BOY BILLIONAIRES Series
To Tame a Tycoon
Sweet Seduction
Daddy by December
To Catch a Man (in 30 Days or Less)
Bedding Her Billionaire Boss
Her Indecent Proposal
So Much Trouble When She Walked In
Married by Midnight
Bad Boy Billionaires - Collection II, Vols. 5 - 8
Bad Boy Billionaires Mega-Collection Vols 1 - 12

THE BILLIONAIRE BROTHERHOOD
Tamed by the Billionaire (Roman's Story)
Maid in the USA (Pierce's Story)
Billionaire's Captive Island Bride (Dare's Story)
Dangerous Deception (Storm's Story)

Romancing Malone
Comedy, Confict & Romance - The Collection

The Naughty and Nice Series
Naughty by Nature

Standalone
The Billionaire's Bold Bet

Watch for more at judyangelo.blogspot.com.

About the Author

New York Times & USA Today best-selling author, Judy Angelo, considers herself a 'traveling writer'. She currently resides in Ontario, Canada but prior to that she called New York and then Illinois home. She has also spent considerable time in the Caribbean, Latin America and Europe. She loves to travel as it provides her with interesting and diverse settings for her stories.

Judy fell in love with romance novels as a teenager and has never lost her passion for these stories of love and life, conflict and reconciliation, relationships and family. For her, it was a natural progression from reading romance novels to writing them. So far, she has written over 70 romance novels, including the best-selling Bad Boy Billionaires series. Her other series include The Billionaire Brothers Kent, The Castillos, and the Comedy, Conflict & Romance series.

She hopes to continue entertaining her readers with intriguing stories for many years to come.

Website - www.judyangelo.blogspot.com

I would love to hear from you! judyangeloauthor@gmail.com

Read more at judyangelo.blogspot.com.